Beautiful, Dirty, Rich

Also by J. D. Mason

J. D. Mason

Beautiful, Dirty, Rich

St. Martin's Press ⚏ New York

This is a work of fiction. All of the characters, organizations, and events portrayed in this novel are either products of the author's imagination or are used fictitiously.

Design by Kathryn Parise

ISBN 978-0-312-61727-1

Dedicated to
Martyrs and bad guys everywhere

Acknowledgments

It's scary writing a brand-new book with brand-new characters, especially when you've become known for a storyline that people have fallen in love with. All sorts of questions come to mind: Will my audience enjoy the story? Will they connect to these characters the way they did with my other characters? Can I really create an entire series from this first book? What will *Publishers Weekly* say?

The struggle with writing *Beautiful, Dirty, Rich* came from trying to write a story that lived up to the boldness of the title. In this case, it was the title that came first and everything else followed. I knew that I wanted to write high drama, and I wanted to write a story about the underdog who comes out on top in the end. But I didn't want to make it easy, or pretty, or nice. My heroine is not easy, pretty, or, deep down, as nice as she appears to be on the surface, and with good reason.

Team BDR has rallied around this book in a big way, and I hope that readers will rally around it, too. At the top of my gratitude list for this project is of course my editor, Monique Patterson, who has the patience of a saint, the insight of a mystic, and the rah-rah-sis-boom-bah of the cheerleader at the top of the pyramid! She's the bee's knees, the cat's meow, and a whole list of other catchy sayings which, if I could remember all of them, would make up their own chapter.

My agent and friend, Sara Camilli, is what Angelo Dundee was to Muhammad Ali. I call her up sometimes just to chat, because she is my friend, and that's the kinds of things good friends do. She keeps me going when I don't feel like I should, and for that I am eternally grateful.

Holly Blanck! Monique's right and left hand, and my go-to girl who keeps me on track and moving forward—thank you for being there, and know that even though you have probably never heard me say it, I appreciate you!

Loren Jaggers, my brand-new publicist, who came to the squad rocking and rolling already, thank you in advance for all of your support and fine introduction. I am looking forward to working together for a very long time, and I'm confident already that if anybody can turn me into an A-list, superstar author, you can!

Carleen Brice and Kim R. Reid, thank you for our monthly luncheons and alcohol powwows. I don't know what I would do if I didn't have you two to bitch to, to laugh and cry with, and to drink with when this business really beats us up. We're in this together, the Three Musketeers! Hooooorah!

Beautiful, Dirty, Rich

Beautiful, Dirty, Rich

Mary, Mary

Mary Travis had sold her soul, but by the time she'd repented for it, it was already too late. She'd taken the money.

The girl is young, she'd told herself back then. *She's strong, and she'll have plenty of time to build a life for herself and to start over again in twenty-five years. God takes care of fools and children. Surely, that girl is no exception.* But Mary had still taken the money.

Not a day went by that she wasn't tormented by the fear that she'd seen in that child's eyes.

"Momma? Momma!" The sound of her crying and calling out to her mother that day in that courtroom tortured Mary to this day, and broke her heart all over again. And even now, as she lay on the floor of her parlor feeling her life slowly begin to slip away from her, knowing that she was about to come face-to-face with God or the devil, Mary's thoughts were not on herself, but on that girl.

God washed away sins, and he forgave the sinner, but not all sins, and not all sinners. Her face would be the last one Mary ever saw, but of course, the image of the girl had always been lurking in the shadows of Mary's mind, waiting patiently for a fair and equitable retribution.

Mary tasted blood in her mouth. Her throat had closed up until it was impossible to breathe or to cry out. Panic flooded her mind and body as she lay motionless on the floral rug in her small parlor room, staring at the wheels of her wheelchair that had rolled to the other side of the room. A warm, thick liquid pooled around her cheek. Mary blinked; it was the only movement she could make. A tear streamed down the side of her face, as she heard crying coming from someplace else in that room.

She desperately needed to take a breath. Mary's heart beat feverishly, echoing in her ears until it was almost deafening. For years she'd waited to die. For years, life had tortured her, bringing her half a breath short of death, only to allow her one more miserable day to suffer in her guilt. She should've been afraid, but she wasn't. This time, she wouldn't pull through. This time, there wouldn't be any miracles. She was done.

She had known all along that she deserved to be punished for the part she'd played in this. *Jesus! Forgive me!* she pleaded in her mind.

But you took the money, Mary, a haunting voice answered her. *You still took the money.*

As the other woman stepped over Mary, the sound of sobbing stabbed Mary's heart, causing it to break even more.

Don't you cry for me! she wanted to shout. *Don't you dare!*

Beware lest you lose the substance
by grasping at the shadow.
—Aesop

A Girl and a Dream

"*Desi Green's* story really is stranger than fiction, Jeremy," Sue Parker explained walking alongside her editor, Jeremy Kennedy, through the lunchtime-crowded streets of Midtown Manhattan. "And it would make a great read."

"It's okay," he said dismissively, "but there are other stories, more recent stories that people actually remember, Sue." She'd been trying to talk him into letting her write this story for months, and he'd stonewalled her. "You're talking about a murder that took place nearly thirty years ago. No one cares."

He was right, of course. Sue Parker made her living writing books about the lives and times of ax murderers, child killers, and flesh-and-blood grim reapers, all of whom had committed their crimes years after Desi Green was sentenced for murdering a millionaire. Sue was known for telling the gruesome truth in her books, the no-holds-barred details of murder straight from the psycho's mouth. Desi's story, by comparison to what she was used to writing, was tame. But her motivation for wanting to write it was coming from another place.

"Okay, so she shot her mother's lover and went to prison for it. No big deal, I know."

"Then stop trying to pitch it to me if you know. It's dull."

"I don't think it is, Jeremy," she argued. "And I don't want to write about the murder. I want to write about her."

"Let me say this slowly." He stopped, took hold of her by the shoulders, and turned her to face him. "Nobody cares."

"Women would care," she shot back quickly. "The number of women in prison has grown by over eight hundred percent in the past three decades. That's almost twice the number of men, Jeremy."

"Then find a woman serial killer to write about," he said indifferently.

"Have you ever seen her?"

He let her go and started walking back to his office. "Not lately."

"She was little more than a kid when they sent her to prison, Jeremy. And not much older than your daughter."

He cut his eyes at her, and quickened his pace. "My daughter hasn't shot anybody lately, Sue. I think you can stop trying to woo me with Desi Green by comparing the two."

"She grew up in prison," she continued, doubling her steps to keep pace with him. "What was that like? What did growing up in a place like that do to her, and what kind of woman is she now?"

"It's touching. Real tug-at-the-old-heartstrings kind of touching, Sue, but uninteresting."

"While she was in prison, her mother died. Can you imagine what it must've been like for her to come home knowing that the woman she loved more than anything was no longer part of this world?"

"You've got half a block to convince me that this conversation is worth my time," he said curtly. "And so far, you're failing miserably."

"Has she ever had a date? Kissed a guy? Made love to one? She's in her forties now. How does she feel about the possibility of never having children?"

"Pity," he said irritably. "My answer is still no."

"Twenty million dollars, Jeremy." She stopped walking.

He stopped too, and slowly turned to her.

"Desi Green, ex-con, felon, murderer, is worth twenty million dollars." He tilted his head curiously to one side. "How'd that happen?"

She smiled, and folded her arms across her chest. "If you'd been paying attention, you'd know."

She could see the wheels start to spin behind his eyes. "Gatewood money?"

Sue nodded. "By way of momma bear. The woman was loaded, courtesy of that beautiful, dirty, rich bastard, Julian Gatewood. She never spent a dime of that money. And when she died, it all went to Desi."

He took a step toward her. "Am I correct in assuming that the Gatewoods are pretty pissed about it?"

"Uber pissed. They hate her now more than ever."

He nodded introspectively. "Hate. That's good. Hate and millions of dollars and a dead man, that's even better."

"It's downright scandalous," she said, smugly.

"Uber scandalous."

"It's the layers I want to peel back, Jeremy," she explained. "On the surface, there's nothing here that anyone cares about. But I have a feeling," she pressed her hand to her stomach, "here. And you know how right on the money my gut instinct can be."

He thought before finally responding. "I'll have to try and get it past Mark."

Mark was the publisher.

"Can you write me a riveting pitch?"

She reached into her purse and pulled out a large manila envelope. "I thought about mailing it, but thought you'd be more impressed if I hand delivered it, myself."

A spark twinkled in his brown eyes. "I am."

"This story's got it all, Jeremy. Drama, loss of innocence, heartache, money, and if my gut instinct is any indication, there's a really good mystery here too."

"I'll see what I can do," he said, turning to leave.

Sue took a deep breath, and let it out slowly. This book would be different from anything else she'd ever written. In the past, Sue had basically been a reporter. She investigated, interviewed, and simply typed down what she was told. She'd always kept herself emotionally detached from the beasts she'd interviewed. After all, what in the world could she possibly have in common with serial killers? But there was something about Desi Green that intrigued her. Desi was everywoman, whose life had changed on a dime. Before that night, there was nothing extraordinary about that teenage girl. She had never been in trouble at school or with the police. The old news footage she'd seen of Desi during the trial struck a chord with Sue. Desi's innocent face, the terror and confusion in her eyes had captivated her. Sue had read through the trial transcripts half a dozen times, and never did anyone mention motive.

If a girl's gonna shoot a guy . . . of course, she's got to have a reason. Desi had never gone on record to say what her reason could've been, and no one, it seemed, had ever bothered to ask.

Blink, Texas

The porch still creaked. When Desi Green had moved out of this old place, she hadn't even bothered to lock the door because she knew that nobody was crazy enough to go inside. Desi pushed open the front door and stepped inside to the small living room. The musty smell was overwhelming, blanketing her in the past.

Not all of her memories of this place were bad, though. Desi had found that if she stood still long enough, sometimes one of the good ones would come into focus and almost make her smile. This time was no exception. Desi closed the door behind her, stood there, and waited as the haunting crescendo of James Brown began to rise up in the corner of the living room where that old record player used to be.

Across the room the sofa came into view, and Desi saw the image of her mother begin to take shape, as Ida Green laughed and clapped, light twinkled in her eyes. Finally, she saw him, Mr. J, Julian Gatewood, twirling around the room in an expensive gray suit, crisp white shirt, and navy blue-and-gold-striped tie, dancing the boogaloo, as he called it. Finally, she saw herself, the little girl Desi, spinning around him like a top, doing her own rendition of a dance that she could never do as well as he.

"You got it." He laughed. *"That's it, Desi! You boogalooing, girl!"*

And she was.

He was tall and handsome, and expensive looking, with golden hair and blue eyes. He looked like a white man to Desi. She'd even told him that once to his face. He got mad, but the only reason she knew he was mad was because he turned red in the face, just like white people did, but he never raised his voice to her.

"I'm as black as you, little girl," he said.

"But you got eyes like white people and hair like 'em too."

"Desdimona!" her mother yelled from the kitchen. *"What'd I tell you 'bout bein' so mannish?"*

Mr. J put his hand up to let Ida know that he could handle an eight-year-old just fine without her help.

"Black people in this country come in all shades and shapes and sizes, Desi," he explained. *"One drop."* He held up one long finger to make his point. *"That's all it takes. One drop of black blood makes a person black, and I promise you,"* he chuckled, *"I've got a whole lot more in me than just a drop coursing through my veins."*

She'd always called him Mr. J, and it wasn't until the trial that she learned his real name. It wasn't until the trial that she learned he had another family, a wife, kids. That's when she found out that he didn't belong to Desi and her mother, Ida. The two of them had only borrowed him.

James Brown's screams turned into her own. Desi wasn't a little girl anymore. She had just turned eighteen. The pop! pop! sound of a gun being fired filled the room. Desi watched in fascination and horror as Mr. J stopped dancing the boogaloo, stared at her with wide and unbelieving eyes, put his hand to his chest, and dropped slowly to his knees onto the floor. Blood seeped through his white shirt and fingers. No more boogalooing. No more dancing. No more happy memories.

Twenty-six years had passed since that night. And in all those years, Desi had learned two things, that obsession was a bitch and money was everything. She'd come to see and to know the power of both firsthand because she'd spent the last twenty-six years of her life smothered by them.

He wasn't the only one who had died in this house. Years later, while Desi wasted away in prison, her mother, Ida Fay Green, died here too. And even if you didn't believe in ghosts, it was hard not to see them in this place. After her release, Desi had no place else to go but here. And what was left of Mr. J and her mother haunted her every single moment that she stayed.

Her mother's room was empty now but she remembered it exactly as it had been before they took her away in handcuffs. The bed was always perfectly made, covered in a pastel yellow bedspread and laced pillows. Ida loved to smell good and rows of half-empty bottles of perfume lined the top of her dresser, along with tubes of lipstick and powder.

"We regret to inform you that your mother passed away of a heart attack, Miss Green," the warden had told her. Desi was twenty years into her prison sentence. The Warden waited for Desi's reaction. Desi blinked, and forced herself to remember how to breathe. Her mother's face came into view in her mind, but it didn't last. Ida had been her anchor to the world outside prison and the Warden had just told her that her anchor was gone. Desi had no words. No tears. She didn't have anything anymore.

She picked up a dusty photograph lying on the floor of twelve-year-old Desi and Ida. Desi blew off the dust, and smiled. Growing up, she never thought she looked like her mother, but now it was hard to miss the resemblance. Desi was as tall as Ida, or as short, depending on your perspective. Ida was a petite woman, five-two, five-three, with full curves, soft brown eyes, a warm smile, and thick black hair that most people believed was a wig. Ida had been that unassuming kind of pretty that could easily be overlooked if you didn't pay attention.

Desi had sold this house for next to nothing to a young couple from out of town who weren't afraid of ghosts. It had taken everything in her to finally let it go, but if she was going to move on with her life, then selling the house was a good place to start.

Blink, Texas was a small enough town that he couldn't help but drive past this old place from time to time. Ida Green's house had been shut up tight until her daughter, Desi, moved back in. But she had moved out of it as soon as she had gotten all of that money, and slapped a FOR SALE sign up in the front yard before the ink had dried on that check. Of course, nobody who knew the history wanted anything to do with the place, so it wasn't surprising when some folks from out of town snatched it up for almost free.

He'd heard gossip that she was back. Desi Green had pulled into town driving one of those fancy European convertible sports cars like she was a movie star or something. But unlike everyone else in town, Tom Billings was just curious. That's all. Curious to see how money could change a convicted felon into whatever she was now. The two of them had a history that went beyond both of them being born and raised in Blink, Texas. He'd never mistreated her, though, despite what she might've thought at the time. He had been firm, but never abusive. Ultimately, everything had worked out for that girl in the end. In a strange way it had worked out for her better than it had for anybody else.

"Desi." He stood in the front yard and greeted her as she was coming out of the house.

She'd just closed the door and stood on the porch, staring down at him. Tom didn't like that.

"Heard you were in town." He smiled.

She looked good. Real good. She looked rich and nearly brand new. Desi Green had a few years on her now the same way they all did, but she didn't look the same way she had when she first moved back here. Standing there in some of those skinny jeans that all the women wore nowadays, and high heels, wearing fancy sunglasses, she did look like she ought to live in Hollywood. Her long, pretty hair, thick and glossy black hung loose and straight, past her shoulders. She looked so much like Ida, only fancier.

"Sheriff Billings." She crossed her arms and curled her lips at the corners, making it clear that she wasn't happy to see him.

He chuckled. "Nobody's called me sheriff in years, Desi. I'm retired now." He waited for her to respond, but she didn't. She just looked at him.

"Sold the house, I see." He motioned his head toward the obvious SOLD sticker across the front of the sign.

She shifted her weight from one expensive shoe to the other. Gone was that shy and awkward teenager, so full of tears and fear. And gone was that insecure and confused woman fresh out of the pen. Tom had been a cop for forty years and he prided himself on his prowess for observation. He'd always been good at reading people. That Desi Green, the younger one, the poorer one, was the one he liked. This one—he didn't know what to make of.

"Is there something I can do for you?"

Her tone threw him off balance. Tom was sensitive to the tone of voice people took when they spoke to him. He shook it off this time.

Life hadn't been fair to that girl when she was younger. Obviously, he thought, looking her up and down, it had taken a turn for the better. "You doing alright?" he asked. "You happy now?" He waited for an answer but didn't get one. "The Lord worked things out in your favor. From dead last to first place." He laughed. "I'd call that a blessing."

She stared down at him and Tom began to feel uncomfortable standing at the bottom of those stairs. She had the advantage, visually, strategically, and in more ways than he cared to admit to. But he couldn't give in and let her know that.

"So, you came here to tell me how blessed I am?" Desi asked, unemotionally.

He didn't like her attitude. "I came to see about you, that's all."

Desi took a fearless step forward. "What's there to see?"

It was too bad that he was a retired cop. It was too damn bad.

"It wasn't that long ago when this house was all you had, Desi," he said, coolly. "Sometimes a person gets so caught up in where they are that they forget where they came from." His tone turned menacing. "I know you have more now than you used to," he chose his words carefully, "and I'm happy that things turned around for you the way they did, but don't forget how you came by it."

"Everything I have, Sheriff, I got from my mother."

"Who got it from the man you killed, Desi," he said, reminding her of that part of the truth that she'd conveniently left out.

"Doesn't matter." She stared defiantly at him. "I got it honestly."

Was she being sarcastic or disrespectful? "I'm here to tell you to be careful and don't ever take what you have for granted, because just as easily as you got it, it could be gone." He snapped his fingers. "Just like that."

She slowly descended the steps. "I was a kid the last time somebody took anything from me," she said threateningly. "And I don't plan to let it happen again."

He glared at her as she walked past him toward her car.

"Careful, girl," he warned. "I'm retired, not dead."

Desi stopped with her back to him. "I'm not dead anymore either, Tom."

Desi climbed in behind the wheel of her ghost-gray Aston Martin, revved the engine, and smiled at him one last time before finally backing out of the driveway. He watched her disappear down the road and turn the corner. Having money, Gatewood money, had gone to her head and it had made a fool out of the rest of them. "Take the money and run, Desi Green," he muttered. "You just go on."

My Soul, Sistah

A million dollars buys a lot of house in Texas. Too bad it had nothing in it. The only piece of furniture she'd bought since she'd had the place built was a king-sized bed. So, Desi confined herself to sitting on a blanket spread out on the floor in her massive living room.

"You can take the girl out of prison, but you can't take the prison out of the girl."

Coming from anybody else, a statement like that would've hurt Desi's feelings. But Lonnie wasn't just anybody.

Yolanda "Lonnie" Adebayo was a year younger than Desi, and when Desi was sent to the pen, Lonnie sent her a letter out of the blue, and just that quick, Desi, the convicted murderer had a fan.

Dear Desi,

I've never written to a prisoner before. I live in Omaha and I saw you on the news. You remind me of a girl in my biology class and you looked scared.

I'd be scared too if I were you, but you are not alone. I feel bad for you and will be praying long and hard for God to watch over you. I know you had to have a reason for doing what you did. But he probably deserved it. I don't expect for you to write me back. I just wanted you to know that there is somebody out here who is on your side no matter what.

Stay strong!

Lonnie

Desi did write her back.

I didn't know that what's happening here was on the news all the way in Omaha. I appreciate your prayers and your letter. The only thing I can tell you is that, to me, he didn't deserve to die. But what I say doesn't matter. So I try not to say anything.

Lonnie was the outgoing one, the one that lived her life to the fullest, who took chances. She wasn't afraid of anything or anyone and shared every private and forbidden detail of her life with Desi through her letters.

Dear Desi,

So I finally hooked up with James, and it really wasn't all that. That boy kisses like a fish. Too much spit and he had no idea what to do with his tongue. It was all over the place, girl. But that's okay, because I met his friend Steven and Steven saw me and I think that he's probably a much better kisser than James. I'll let you know as soon as I find out.

Dear Desi,

Prom night! Remember Isaac? I went with him and I finally got laid. It hurt, but I think I'm going to like it.

Dear Desi,

I got accepted into Cornell University in Ithaca, New York. Momma doesn't want me to move that far away, but I can't wait to get out of Omaha. The world is bigger than Nebraska. I keep trying to tell her that. She looks at me like I'm an alien from another planet. I feel sorry for her.

Dear Desi,

Todd proposed, but I turned him down. I don't think he'll ever talk to me again, but it's a relief if he doesn't. We're too young to get married, and he's made it clear that he wants a house full of babies. Kids are cool—other people's kids are cool. Marriage and babies sound like they'd be heavy and you know me. I like to travel light.

It got to where Desi not only looked forward to hearing from Lonnie, but she came to depend on those letters. She could escape her surroundings through Lonnie's letters. Desi experienced everything that Lonnie did, from what it felt like to get accepted into and to graduate from college, to the joy of getting her first *real* paycheck from her first *real* job, and even the pain and pleasure of falling in and out of love.

Lonnie wrote regularly, except when life got in the way and she was too busy living it to think about stopping long enough to write to anybody. Those times were the hardest times for Desi, waiting and wondering if maybe Lonnie had had enough, and had decided that she'd outgrown Desi. But eventually, Lonnie came through like a champ and wrote page after page of every single thing that had happened to her since the last time she'd written.

A few days before Desi was to be released, Lonnie wrote asking for

Desi's address in Blink, Texas. A month after Desi made it home, Lonnie knocked on the front door and officially introduced herself.

"I got a place in Dallas," she'd told Desi. Dallas was about a hundred miles northeast of Blink. "I would've found a place here in town, but—" She turned up her nose. "I'm just not a Blink, Texas, kind of girl, you understand."

Seeing Lonnie poured into those expensive jeans, stiletto thigh-high boots, and silk blouse, Desi nodded. "Oh, yeah. I understand."

Less than a year later, Lonnie lay sprawled out on the floor in Desi's expensive living room. Desi leaned back against the wall. Between them was a nearly empty pizza box with a couple of half eaten slices left. On the floor around them were two empty beer bottles, and what was left of a bottle of Patrón Silver tequila.

Lonnie was five-eight and shapely, with smooth, dark skin, and a smart bold fade that complimented beautiful high cheekbones and almond eyes. Her exotic features reminded Desi of someone who should've come from someplace in Africa instead of Nebraska.

Lonnie's unconventional beauty turned heads everywhere she went, and she played up her image wearing bright colors, huge earrings, and six-inch heels, making sure to leave the kind of indelible impression in people's memories long after she'd left the room.

Tonight she wore a simple maxi sundress, covered in pretty yellow daisies. Desi had on a pair of black, Capri leggings, and a white tank top. To anybody on the outside looking in, they were just two friends, hanging out together and getting drunk on the living room floor. And neither one of them had spent more than half of her life in prison.

"I heard from my friend today," Lonnie said, rolling over on her side to face Desi. "The one that works for the city."

Lonnie had friends in high places, and friends of friends who had friends in high places.

"Yeah? What'd he say?" Desi slurred.

"Well, the place does have an address. It didn't just sprout up from the ground like a rose bush." She laughed.

"It's a business?"

Lonnie shrugged. "Don't know. But he gave me the name and number of the owner. It's in my purse."

Lonnie was a photojournalist, but not just any photojournalist. She didn't just take pictures of weddings or babies. Lonnie traveled the world, snapping pictures of everyone from the queen of England to war-torn cities in the Middle East. Her stories and pictures had been published in *Time* magazine, *Life* magazine, and she'd even gotten one photo of a prominent politician sitting at a stoplight and kissing on a woman who wasn't his wife. Lonnie had framed that one and proudly displayed it in her living room. A few weeks after she took it, the scandal about his infidelity broke, and eventually he had to step down from his position.

Of the two of them, Desi gave Lonnie credit for being smarter, and she knew every damn body. Through the years, they'd become not only friends, but best friends, which was odd considering the circumstances of how they met.

Lonnie was the one who knew how to look at something objectively to analyze a situation and find the solution to the problem. She was the one who solved puzzles when all Desi could see were pieces scattered all over the place. Lonnie could pick out opportunity in a mountain of bullshit, and make something out of nothing. She knew how to take the jumbled chaos of everything Desi felt, and put some order to it. And she gave Desi permission to cry, curse, and scream without condemning her.

So when Desi casually explained a brief encounter she'd had recently with someone from her past, Lonnie's eyes lit up like high beams.

"I'd just finished meeting with the realtor at the old house and was on my way back to Dallas when I saw the judge that presided over my trial, Judge Fleming," she explained to Lonnie one afternoon over coffee.

"You hadn't seen him since you went to prison?"

Desi shook her head. "He looked as old now, as he did back then. Like time had stood still for him."

"How'd it feel to see him again, Desi?"

She paused before answering. "It scared me, Lonnie. It scared me just as much to see him now as it did to sit in the courtroom across from him back then. I felt like if he saw me, he could sentence me all over again."

"Any other judge sitting up here on this bench would give you the death penalty. You should thank God that I'm not any other judge."

"He stopped at the light and I pulled up alongside him. I don't know why I did that, but, I couldn't stop looking at him. I couldn't take my eyes off him."

"Did he see you?"

"He glanced at me, but he didn't act like he knew who I was. When the light turned green and he pulled away, I followed him."

Lonnie's eyes widened. "Why?"

Desi shrugged. "I don't know. I just . . . I don't know what I expected to happen or where I expected him to go. Even if he just went to his house, I had no idea what I would do when he parked. I just did it."

Desi explained how she followed him on a stretch of road leading into the next county, and how he nearly ran off the road at one point.

"I think he must've known that I was following him. I think he almost ran into that ditch because he saw me behind him."

"So you think he did recognize you?"

"Maybe."

The judge sped up, but Desi was careful not to. Eventually, he slowed down and turned off onto a dirt road, but Desi kept going.

"I doubled back," she explained.

"Where'd you think he was going, Desi?" Lonnie asked, concerned.

"I don't know, Lonnie, but I went back and turned down that same road. It didn't look like it led to anywhere. I thought I was going to drop off into some ravine or something."

She drove for a few miles before she finally stopped and saw a one story, brick building, surrounded by tall trees, and the judge's car parked out front. He'd stood by and watched as the valet, or whoever it was, drove away in his car, and then he walked up to the door and waited to be let inside.

Lonnie's curiosity was on fire. "Was there a sign on the building? An address that you could see?"

"Nothing. Not even windows. But quite a few cars were parked on the back side of it, and when the judge went inside, I heard music."

Lonnie leaned back and relaxed. "A good ol' boy's club," she said, sighing. "Did you go up and knock on the door?" Lonnie asked the question, knowing the answer already.

Desi looked surprised. "Of course not."

Lonnie was disappointed. "Still afraid of the big, bad, wolf, I see."

Desi stared at her. "Something like that."

She told Lonnie about the place and where it was. Lonnie contacted her friend who had a friend working in the County Planning Office, and now she had an address and the name of the owner.

Desi stared at the piece of paper Lonnie had pulled out of her purse and handed to her.

"What am I supposed to do with this?" she said, tossing back another shot of tequila.

Lonnie was her usual cool and unflustered self. "You're going to call the owner and ask him or her about the property at that address. Maybe tell them you came across it and you're interested in buying it."

"It's not that serious," Desi said, tossing the paper aside.

Lonnie picked it up. "Old judges don't drive down dirt roads to go to unmarked buildings in the middle of the afternoon for nothing, Des. He's hiding something. I feel it in my bones."

"Even if he is, what's that got to do with me?"

Lonnie stared, stone faced. "I can't believe you just asked me that."

"So what are you implying, Lonnie? That I should dig up dirt on that old mother fucker and what?"

Lonnie sighed. "You expect me to give you the answers to the test, Desi? Really?"

"I don't give a damn about what that old fool was doing out there in the middle of the woods. How's that?"

"Then why the hell did you follow him?"

"To see . . . him! It wasn't about anything else but to look at him, and to see him. I still had that picture of him in my head that was twenty-six years old. I guess I was hoping to see something different."

"I see an opportunity, Desi. That's how my mind works. Every scenario, every situation, is an opportunity to discover something more."

"More what?"

"Could be nothing. Could be a bunch of old men sitting around in a room, playing poker, smoking cigars, drinking, and getting laid by a few, down-on-their-luck, working girls." She shrugged. "No big deal. But, my instinct tells me that it could be something else. What if it is?"

"I don't care. Even if it is more than that, what the hell do you expect me to do?"

Lonnie just stared at her. "I swear. Sometimes, I feel like I'm the hardened criminal in this duo. Open your eyes, girl! With everything you've been through, don't you ever want to lash out and get back at those bastards? You did it with Mary!"

"I didn't touch her! I did not lay a finger on her!"

"No, you didn't. But you didn't exactly call 9-1-1 either when she fell. Did you?"

Angry tears filled Desi's eyes.

"Why didn't But?" Lonnie challenged. "I know why? And deep down, so do you."

Desi braced herself against the wall and stood up. "We've had too much to drink," she slurred. "You want some pie?" She stumbled into the kitchen.

"One down, Desi. All I'm saying is that you've got the momentum in your favor, the wind's against your back. I believe in karma, and I don't believe in accidents. You saw him for a reason, and you followed him for a reason."

Desi sat back down with a whole sweet potato pie, and two forks. "What's done is done. I need to move on!" She dug into the pie with her fork. "I can't change what happened, Lonnie. But, I got paid, so . . ."

"Is that all it takes, Des? A little money and it's all good? Twenty-five years of your life gone, eaten away like termites eat wood, and that's it? Get out of jail and buy yourself a pair of Jimmy Choos and a gold watch for time served? You really believe that?"

"I want to believe that." She tried swallowing the pie she'd shoved into her mouth.

"But you know, deep down, it's not true."

Desi and Lonnie locked gazes.

"He didn't know who you were?"

Desi shook her head. "I don't think he did."

"He didn't know, because you never meant shit to him. He washed his hands of you the minute they hauled you out of his courtroom."

A tear streamed down Desi's cheek. "It doesn't matter."

Lonnie scooted closer to her and drove her fork into the pie. "This looks good."

Lonnie's dark eyes locked onto Desi's and dared her to turn away. "The difference between Desi now and Desi twenty-six years ago, is money. Lots of money and freedom. The difference between that bastard and you, is that he washed his hands of you as soon as he slammed that gavel down and they took you away. You on the other hand, can't let it go, Desi. You can try to lie to yourself, but you can't lie to me. I see it in you. I feel the pain of what you've been through."

"But I got mine, Lonnie." Desi swallowed. "I've gotten the money. I've gotten my inheritance."

"That money can never buy back what he took from you, Desi, and you know it. You lost a lifetime. You can't put a price on that, Des. People like him want you to believe that you'll take the money and run so that he can rest a little bit better at night thinking that you've somehow been repaid for your services, and it eases his conscience. But you know the truth, even if you don't want to admit it out loud. You hate him. You hate him for what he did to you."

Unexpected tears fell from her eyes. "So, I hate him. What good does that do? It eats me up, but it doesn't mean shit to people like him."

"Then make it mean something," Lonnie said, carefully. "Don't let him rest easy. Let him know that you aren't going to let him make you just another unpleasant memory, and that you're not going to crawl off to a corner and curl up and die without making a fuss."

"What are you talking about?"

The magic of Lonnie was her fearlessness, her willingness to go wherever she needed to go to do whatever she needed to do.

"You get even, Desi!"

Desi looked at her and laughed. "You watch too many soap operas, Lonnie. People don't do that shit in real life."

"People with money do. Your pockets are deeper than his, Desi. You've got the resources to find the dirty, if you look hard enough."

"You really think that's going to make me feel better? You think that finding shit on him will make up for what he did to me?"

Lonnie nodded. "I think it could be a good place to start."

Beauty

Seventy-year-old Olivia Gatewood poured cream into her tea, dropped two cubes of sugar into it, leaned back in her chaise, and gazed out over the expanse of her property. She had always lived a privileged life, and most times, she took it for granted. For years, she'd felt herself slipping away, fading like an old photograph, and because of that, she made certain to pay close attention to the small things that meant the most to her, like the view from the window of her bedroom, the scent of her favorite flowers, the feel of silk against her skin, and memories, which she tried to recapture in her journal to save and relive again when they lost the vividness of color.

Occasionally glancing at her bedroom door, she worked hard to quell the anticipation of seeing him walk through it nearly thirty years after his death. Her gaze drifted over to the clock sitting on the mantel of the fireplace. Four o'clock. Julian came home every day at four. She sipped her tea, but then gradually began to give in to worry as the minutes ticked away. That familiar anxious knot blossomed in her stomach. *Come home to me,* she pleaded in her thoughts. He was a prompt man, a regimented man. Julian was never late except when he—Ten after four. Olivia carefully placed her teacup down on the table, leaned back in her chair, and retreated into her memories.

That small corner of northeast Texas was a big, small town. She and Ida Green had met years before in an encounter too insignificant to matter until years later, the night Julian died. The first time she'd ever laid eyes on Ida, the two of them were just girls. Back then, Olivia didn't know her name, and she didn't care to know it. They had no relationship, other than that of patron and clerk. She'd crossed through two towns to get a tear on a dress mended to keep her parents from finding out that it had been ripped in the first place by a boy too zealous for his own good.

Henthorne, Texas, where she lived, wasn't as small as Blink, but it was small enough and people had a tendency to gossip, even about something as insignificant as a torn dress. Being that Olivia's father was the first and only colored doctor in Bond County, made her name very popular in gossip circles, and all sorts of stories would've been manufactured as to how her expensive dress managed to get ripped down the side seam at the zipper, before the seamstress in Henthorne had even handed her a receipt. So, she took it to Blink. Nobody knew her in Blink.

The darker woman behind the counter examined the material, and then looked up at Olivia over the rims of her reading glasses.

"This is silk," she said, sounding surprised.

"Of course it's silk," Olivia retorted. "The finest silk from India. It's one of a kind, designed just for me, which is why you need to take your time and make sure you don't make a mistake when you fix it."

Thinking back on her candor back then, Olivia couldn't help but smile, and then take a sip of her tea. She'd been eighteen, maybe nineteen, with a sassy mouth that lent itself to getting her all sorts of sideways glances. Olivia's flippancy was excused, though, because of who her father was, and because she was beautiful. She was a lighter-skinned black, with sandy-gold-colored hair that she wore straight, and wrapped with a wide ribbon. Most men stared when they saw her, black or white, it didn't matter. Back then, Olivia was like a beautiful, ripe apple, hanging from the highest branch at the top of the tallest tree, that all men wanted, but none of them could reach. And she knew it.

Olivia was concerned that the woman wouldn't be able to mend silk, when a younger version of the woman pushed through the door and lumbered into the room to the other side of the counter. She stood next to the older version of herself, placing a package on top of the counter. She didn't so much as glance at Olivia or excuse herself before she started talking.

"Miss Parker only had three yards left of the fabric you wanted, Momma." The girl disappeared through the small doorway behind her mother.

A long rope of hair hung down one of the girl's shoulders across her breast.

"Where's my change, Ida Fay?" her mother called out.

"She didn't give me any," the girl said. "She said we owed her money, so she kept it."

"Was that a hairpiece?" Olivia suddenly asked, enviously. Of course it had to have been a hairpiece.

The seamstress shot a look at her. "No. That's her hair." The woman almost sounded offended.

Olivia stared, infuriated, at the woman. She seemed to realize that her tone had been unacceptable quickly, and smiled apologetically to Olivia.

"I can have this mended, just like it was new, by Friday."

The younger girl came back and stood next to her mother behind the counter and traced her fingertips over the expensive fabric. "It's beautiful," she said, under her breath. She shot a shy gaze up at Olivia who stood a head taller.

"My mother ordered it from a famous designer," Olivia said, proudly. "It's from Paris."

The girl batted her eyes, and frowned. "Paris, Texas?"

Olivia rolled her eyes. "Paris, France," she said smugly.

That girl was so simple, and so country. She was so ordinary. But she was harmless, and sweetness resonated from her because she was no threat to Olivia. She was no threat to any woman, really. Olivia walked out of that shop, fairly confident that she'd get her dress back as good as new, and with no thought whatsoever to the girl with the long, braided hair.

"Time for your medication, Mrs. Gatewood." Abby, her day nurse sat down across from her and placed a silver serving tray down on the small table between them.

"My husband was a peculiar man," Olivia said, all of a sudden, to Abby.

The woman smiled, nodded, and handed her a small white cup filled with pills. Olivia poured them into her mouth. Abby handed her a clear glass filled with water and waited patiently for Olivia to sip it and wash down her medication.

"You can never be certain as to what goes on in a man's mind," she continued, staring intensely into Abby's eyes.

"No, ma'am," Abby agreed.

A woman like Ida Green had meant nothing to Olivia the day she'd first met that girl. She hadn't meant a thing to her the day she drove back to Blink to pick up her dress either. They had stood less than a foot from each other, while Ida showed her the place on the dress that had been torn, and how well her mother had repaired it.

"You can't even tell it was ripped," she'd said to Olivia.

Olivia paid the girl and left, and it never occurred to her that she'd ever have reason to see or talk to her ever again.

She sat reflective in her thoughts for several moments. "Can I give you some advice, Abby?"

Abby smiled again, and nodded. "Of course, Mrs. Gatewood. You know your advice is always welcomed."

Sweet Abby, she smiled warmly. "Never take anyone you meet for granted. Never dismiss them or ignore them, but pay attention. Because you never know if they are just passing through your life for a moment, or if they'll play some crucial part in it. God puts people in our path for a reason. And it can be years before you understand why."

Abby thanked her graciously for her words of wisdom and then got up and left. Of course, she was no different than the rest of them. She thought Olivia was crazy. They all did. And maybe she was. But the day she walked out of that shop, it never occurred to her to ask that girl her name. It didn't seem possible that the same man who loved Olivia and made her his wife, would love a woman so seemingly insignificant as the young woman Olivia paid her money to. Or that he would cling so desperately to her, until the very day he—died?

Heavy tears suddenly flooded her eyes. Olivia raised her thin hand to her mouth and gasped, softly. She looked at the clock again. Four twenty. He wasn't coming home. Not tonight. Not ever.

A Day in the Life

Rich and powerful men had enemies. Jordan Gatewood had more than his share, but he'd mastered the art of keeping those enemies closer than he kept his friends. Now, it seemed, he had some unknown foe sending cryptic text messages to his private number.

Your story is getting dusty

Your lies are getting rusty

The message would've been nothing more than a silly rhyme to anyone else. But Jordan knew better than to dismiss it so easily. It was a threat, a warning, and a man in his position didn't get to and stay where he was by ignoring threats.

Whoever it was that sent it and the others before obviously believed that they had something on him, and decided to play games with what they thought they knew. But anybody who knew Jordan, who really knew him, knew better than to fuck with him.

He'd come downstairs from his bedroom to his home office first thing on a Sunday morning before breakfast–to make a phone call.

"It's me. They sent another one."

Frank Mitchell worked for Jordan and was one of the top IT techs at the company. Jordan trusted his discretion.

"Can you meet me at the office?"

"I can meet you there around four."

"Four's fine." Jordan hung up.

He'd asked Frank to try and track the messages to the source.

"Normally, all I'd have to do is to track the messages signal to the nearest tower to pinpoint the location of where it was sent," Frank explained.

"But this isn't normal?"

"It's like the signal's being bounced from tower to tower. Almost as if each word of the text is being transmitted simultaneously from different locations from different phones."

"That's impossible," Jordan said.

"You would think."

Eventually, Jordan changed his private number, but somehow, whoever was sending these messages managed to get that number as well and picked up where they left off, which led him to the only conclusion that made any sense. Someone he knew was sending him this crap.

Marriage was a necessary evil for a man like Jordan. He'd taken over running Gatewood Industries, in name only, after his father died. Jordan was barely out of college where he'd majored in football and girls. The Board of Directors saw him as more of a nuisance than head of his father's corporation, and they treated him accordingly. Back then, the only thing he was good for was his signature. Other people, more experienced than he was, more knowledgeable, and certainly better groomed for managing a multimillion-dollar corporation, made all the business decisions on his behalf. He made the mistake once of complaining to his mother about it, and she had retreated into her home and become little more than a hermit after the trial.

"It's your father's business, Jordan," she explained to him. "Of course he'd want you to run it, but you know as well as I do, that he'd want you to prove that you could. Julian would never hand over something that important to someone he didn't think was qualified."

"How can I prove that I'm qualified if they won't let me?"

She stared blankly at him. "Since when does anyone have to *let* a Gatewood do anything? Julian didn't let anyone tell him he couldn't become one of Texas's wealthiest black men? You don't let anyone tell you that you can't be who your father meant for you to be." He bullied his way to their respect. It had taken years, but now the executive leadership didn't even wipe their asses without his approval.

Marrying Claire five years ago was a business move, one he'd held off making for as long as he could, and one he went into kicking and screaming. With the words "I do," Jordan was transformed from wealthy playboy to responsible corporate CEO. Stock prices rose at the announcement of his engagement, a phenomenon he found laughable.

"Fashion week in New York is next month. We should go."

Claire was the ideal trophy wife, beautiful, classy, and completely void of substance. Conversations with her were like talking to cardboard, so most of the time she talked, and he didn't bother hiding the fact that he wasn't listening. She looked delicious on his arm, spent money like water, and gave a mind-blowing blow job. What more could a man ask for?

"I know you don't like New York, but—"

"I'll have to check my schedule, Claire," Jordan said, turning the pages of his newspaper before she could finish asking her question.

"I haven't even told you what week it is, Jordan," she said, notably offended.

It wasn't New York that he didn't dig. It was being in New York with Claire during fashion week that didn't sound all that appealing.

"More coffee, Mr. Gatewood?" the housekeeper asked, hovering around him with a fresh pot.

"Thank you, Louise." He held up his cup and never bothered to look up from his newspaper.

"Is it my imagination," Claire asked, getting up from her chair and slowly, seductively walking toward him, "or is my husband more interested in the sports page than his wife?"

One long, caramel-colored leg draped across his lap, and Claire made herself comfortable on his crotch, at the breakfast table. Amber, exotic eyes, a golden mane of hair parted on one side and cascading in rivers down her shoulders, a delectable and appealing tongue moistened her lips—another man would've cum already.

Claire put her hands on the back of his neck, and pulled his face to hers, and slipped her velvet tongue into his mouth. Jordan let her, waiting to feel—something. Before the two of them were married, men were lined up in droves vying for Claire's attention. She was the prize at the carnival and when it was all said and done, he was the winner. It didn't take long for him to reach the conclusion that playing the game had meant more to him than winning.

"We can go upstairs," she whispered, caressing the nape of his neck with her thumbs. "We can work on making some babies." She purred.

Claire pushed her perfect hips deep into his crotch. Disappointment quickly shadowed her eyes when she realized that his body wasn't responding the way she'd hoped it would.

Jordan's cell phone rang, giving him a way out of having to deliver a brutal truth to her. That he wasn't in the mood.

"Yes," he said into the phone, staring into her eyes.

Claire's eyes pooled with disappointment as she pulled away from him and left the room.

It was Sunday. Jordan had no other reason to leave the house that afternoon except that he wanted to. Claire wasn't the problem. She'd come into this marriage with her eyes wide open. Jordan had never told her he loved her. He'd made it clear that he had one daughter already, and that he had no intention of having more children. He wasn't the kind of husband who cut the grass, walked the dog, or who would take long walks with her through the park holding her hand. Claire was an image booster. That's all. She was the other person in the picture when he was photographed, the dutiful and beautiful wife by his side at cocktail parties and fund-raisers. Sometimes she understood that, and accepted it. Most times, especially lately, she sadly seemed to want more.

"I swear you must be psychic, woman." Jordan smiled and leaned inside the doorway of Lonnie's condo. The signal was that Lonnie would call him, and when he answered, she'd hang up. Her idea. Not his. "How'd you know I had a Sunday afternoon to spare?"

Lonnie leaned against the door and shrugged. "I felt that vibe coming from you floating on the wind begging me to make that call," she joked. "I just hoped that today wouldn't be the day that you decided to dump me, break my heart, and leave me begging for you to take me back."

She was lovely to him, exotic, sexy with an edge to her that always kept him guessing. And if anyone was going to be doing any begging in this relationship, Jordan was sure that it would be him.

"Me break your heart?" He came inside and closed the door behind him. "We both know that it would be the other way around."

Lonnie was her name, short for Yolanda. And she was everything that Claire wasn't. She wore her hair cut short and natural. She answered the door wearing a white tank top, and faded tattered jeans. The scent of sage filled her apartment, and the sounds of Jill Scott played from her stereo. A book lay casually strewn facedown and open on the coffee table.

"Please tell me that you didn't leave Mrs. Jordan sitting at home by her lonesome," she said sarcastically as she walked past him.

"Like you really give a damn."

He wanted to reach out and grab ahold of her, but Lonnie wasn't the type to be manhandled by anyone. If she wanted you, she came to you.

She sat on the sofa and curled her legs under her. "It could be." She smiled.

Dark almond eyes seductively glossed over him. "There's wine in the kitchen. Help yourself."

Another woman would've offered to get up and pour him a glass. "Would you like some?"

"Yes. I would."

They'd met at the Dallas Urban Center for Boys and Girls at a dedication ceremony. Jordan had paid for the new gym, had been asked to give a speech, and cut into a ribbon. The beautiful woman in the audience looked like she should've been the one having her picture taken.

"Does my heart good to see big business stepping in to help the community." Lonnie approached him after the ceremony and greeted him with some purple concoction in a plastic cup.

"Does my heart good to do it." He smiled, took a sip of his drink, and grimaced. "What is this?"

Lonnie shrugged. "Kool-Aid."

Afterwards, he offered to buy her a drink. She refused, but begrudgingly took his business card. A month later, he got a call.

"I think I've changed my mind," she said, coolly. "Is that offer for a drink still on the table?"

"It is," he said, smiling. "Meet me at Devina's?"

Devina's was a bar a few blocks down from his office.

"How about you meet me at Barney's, instead?"

"Barney's?" He asked, caught off guard by her suggestion. It wasn't Barney's he had a problem with. It was this woman, who seemed to be the one making up the rules to this game, his game.

"It's more discreet," she told him.

Jordan nodded. "Discretion."

"Discretion is gold when you're Jordan Gatewood and you have a wife."

Touché.

"See you at seven," Lonnie told him, and then hung up.

Jordan gazed up admiringly at the exotic woman straddling him. He held handfuls of her voluptuous behind rolling in wide circles on top of him. Full breasts bounced inches from his lips, and his mouth watered at the thought of tasting them. He raised a hand to her back and pulled her closer and wrapped his lips around each of them, savoring them like sweet fruit.

"Mmmmmm," she moaned, luxuriously.

Hot juice from her pussy soaked his balls and the sheets underneath him. Jordan reached up and cupped her head, wrapped an arm around her waist, and rolled her over on the bed onto her back without breaking the rhythm of their lovemaking.

"Shit, Lonnie," he growled, low and deep into her ear. "I'm coming already."

Lonnie squeezed the inner walls of her vagina, and Jordan dove deep into her and exploded.

Jordan left Lonnie's and showed up at his office a little after four. Frank was already there, waiting.

"Sorry to interrupt what's left of your Sunday, Frank," Jordan said, sitting down behind his desk.

"Not a problem. The wife made meatloaf for dinner. I hate her meatloaf. Wanna fire up the laptop for me?" Frank took the phone from Jordan, while they waited for the laptop to load.

Jordan clicked on his e-mail icon. "I've got another one. It's got a file attached."

Frank came around the desk and stood over his shoulder. "It was sent from a bogus e-mail address. Mind if I take over?"

He switched places with Jordan.

"Click on the link," Jordan told him.

"Jordan, no decent IT guy worth his weight in gigabytes would click on a file from an unknown source."

Jordan reached over him, took the mouse, and clicked the link.

CLEAN UP YOUR RAP, YOUR STORY'S GETTING DUSTY

WASH OUT YOUR MOUTH, YOUR LIES ARE GETTING RUSTY

It took several beats before he realized that it was Nina Simone's voice in that recording. An image of an old black-and-white photograph began to fade in on the screen, of a very young and beautiful woman sitting behind the wheel of an old Buick, and of a man leaning against the car with his arms crossed, with a cigarette dangling from the corner of his mouth.

"You recognize those people? They mean anything to you?"

Yes. He recognized them, and yes, they meant plenty to him. "No," Jordan lied. "Can you track it back to a source?"

"I can try," Frank said, sounding defeated. "But whoever's sending this crap, so far, has managed to stay one step ahead of me."

"Only one?" Jordan quipped. "So what's the problem, Frank?"

"It's a big step, Jordan. A very big step. And I may just be out of my league.

Lean On Me

Jordan was the Goliath to Desi's David. On the surface, Goliath was the monster, the unbeatable giant, and David was an underdog, a nobody. The only person in the universe who didn't see it that way, though, was David. The trick, as far as Lonnie was concerned, was getting Desi to understand that her perceived weakness was her greatest strength.

Jordan came into the arena baring talons and teeth, bearing down on Desi like a lion ready to gobble her up. Desi cowered in the presence of him like a frightened and vulnerable slave, crouching in the corner, whimpering and crying. The lion came with lawyers and injunctions roaring with threats and spewing obscenities.

"I don't even want the money," Desi had cried to Lonnie. *"It's not worth it, Lonnie! I've been through enough, and I'm tired of this shit!"*

Lonnie despised weakness. And she sometimes despised Desi for wasting so much energy and time being the victim. She made some calls to a news producer friend of hers in San Francisco who owed her a favor, and a few days later, the cavalry, in the form of two of the best estate attorneys the country had to offer, showed up at Desi's doorstep. All she had to do was sit back and wait for the pennies to literally rain from heaven.

Lonnie stepped out of the shower, wrapped a towel around herself, and went into the kitchen and poured herself a glass of wine. Jordan was a great lay and a good and obedient boy, but then, men were simple. Dangle a moist and eager pussy in front of their faces and they came running, tales wagging, and tongues hanging out. She stretched out on the chaise in her bedroom. Desi needed Lonnie. Poor girl. How she ever made it through twenty-five years in a federal penitentiary was a miracle, because she was a doormat. But it was all good. Lonnie was here to take care of it, and her motivation was simple. She loved Desi. Loved her like a sister. Loved her like . . . Desi needed her. And she would be there for her as long as she did.

Desi wasn't by nature a fighter. Lonnie was the opposite. When she set her sights on something, she hung on like a pit bull, until she got it.

"You're so hard-headed, Lonnie!" her mother used to complain about Lonnie's determination and drive. Her mother could never see past the walls of that old house they lived in, but Lonnie wasn't about to be boxed into that place. A woman should own who she is. She should expand on what everyone else tells her she should be. She should blow the minds of everyone around her, and leave them speechless. That was the code she lived by, and whenever somebody had the nerve to tell her she couldn't do something, Lonnie would flip them the bird, and tell them, "Watch me." Desi needed to learn that. Lonnie would teach her.

Jordan was a wise man and he had good instincts. She had to be careful around him, so careful. To him, Lonnie was a piece of ass that bucked the system and challenged him. She wasn't a Gatewood groupie, willing to jump through hoops to appease him or please him. A man like him didn't know what to do with a woman like her because he'd never had one. That pretty wife of his knew what kind of man she'd married, and because of who he was and what he had, she turned a blind eye to his indiscretions. If Lonnie had been his wife, she'd have cut his dick off and served it up to him on a platter. He was lucky he hadn't met her first.

Jordan was a man with secrets. All rich men had secrets. Lonnie knew it and she went looking for his and found it. It was the kind of secret a man like him would take to the grave, because to do anything else, would mean the end of the world as he knew it.

Your story is getting dusty

Your lies are getting rusty

She smiled and took a sip of wine. "Goliath ain't so bad, Desi," she murmured. "He ain't so big."

What is Taboo?

"*Jesus!* Don't you people ever stop?" Desi asked, exasperated, into the phone. "I don't talk to reporters. I never have!"

"And again, Miss Green, I am not a news reporter," Sue explained. "I'm a true-crime writer. My specialty is books, not news articles."

"I don't talk to true-crime writers, either!" Desi said sarcastically, and she started to hang up on the woman.

"The state of Texas found you guilty of murder, but I don't think it's that simple," Sue blurted out, expecting to hear the line go dead. It didn't. "The state has taken every opportunity to tell their side of the story, Desi. I just want to give you the platform to tell yours."

The only assurance Sue had that Desi hadn't hung up on her was the fact there she wasn't talking to a dial tone.

"It's been twenty-six years," she continued. "You've been through a lot and you've kept quiet. Nobody knows what really happened the night Julian Gatewood was killed, and nobody knows what you've been through."

"Nobody cares."

"I do. And Ida? What was it like for her seeing her daughter . . ."

"Leave my mother out of this!"

"I'm sorry! Please, don't hang up," Sue pleaded. "I'm just saying that she seemed like a lovely woman, Desi," she said, sincerely. "Lovely and broken hearted."

Desi was silent on the other end of the phone.

"More than one life was lost that night, Desi. And more than one family suffered loss. Isn't that true?"

There was a long pause before Desi finally answered. "You want to write a book about loss?" Desi asked, hesitantly.

Sue sighed. "I want to write a book about truth, Desi. All of it."

It was Sue's most passionate and fevered pitch and regardless of the outcome, she owed herself a firm pat on the back for it.

Of course, Desi was reluctant. Reporters from all over the country had flown into Texas and had camped out in front of the police station, the courthouse, and even on her mother's front lawn during that trial. It wasn't until they found out about the money that they came crawling out of the cracks again like roaches.

CONVICTED MURDERER INHERITS
MILLIONS FROM HER VICTIM!

"How's it feel to be a rich woman, Desi?"

"The Gatewoods have said that your inheritance is a slap in the face and another kind of crime. How does that make you feel?"

"Are you going to spend it, Desi? How can you accept that money with a clear conscience?"

Sue had stumbled across the news footage on YouTube. Desi's story wasn't making national headlines like it once did, but at least in the south, the news of her inheritance was a big deal, and had been the perfect selling point for Sue to make her pitch to Jeremy.

Desi never said a word to any of them, and it about ate her alive to keep her mouth shut, but she'd been trained to do just that. If they had any kind of investigative skills at all, they'd know that it wasn't Mr. J's money that she'd inherited. It was Ida's. Mr. J hadn't left Desi a dime. But he'd left Ida Green a trust fund, under the umbrella of an entity called the IG Foundation. He'd been putting money into that trust for years, in small enough amounts to keep from drawing attention to it by board members of his corporation, and his family.

Ida never touched it. She could've, but she never did, and over time, it had accumulated to over twenty million dollars. She left every cent of it to Desi in her will. "I'll bet you could sell snow to an Eskimo," Desi finally said.

Sue laughed. "If I wanted to bad enough, yeah."

Desi started to read off a list of Sue's titles. *"Brother Rob: The Story of the Convent Rapist, See No Evil: The Last Days of Beth Andrews, No Pain, No Gain: Confessions of the Marlborough Serial Killer.* What do you plan on calling my book, Ms. Parker? *Brown Sugar is Sweet: True Confessions of Desi Green?"*

Sue was offended. Obviously, while she was busy begging and pleading Desi Green for this opportunity, she'd been Googled. "Now you're just being ridiculous," Sue snapped.

"No, you're the one being ridiculous for even calling me in the first place about this bullshit."

"Bullshit!" Sue shrieked. "I'm giving you a chance to tell your story, Desi! This is a shot, a shot for you to open your mouth and finally say something, for crying out loud! A chance to speak up for yourself instead of sitting back like a slug and letting everybody else do it for you!"

"You almost sound like you think I'm innocent," Desi said, sarcastically.

Sue couldn't believe she'd just said that. It was a strange thing to say, and even stranger to hear. "Are you?"

Again, there was dead silence on the other end of the phone, but . . . what if?

"I know that your life hasn't been easy," Sue Parker added. "You're trying to make a fresh start. So, why not close out that part of your life by telling your side of the story," Sue said, quickly. "I believe that there's more to your story than meets the eye. I believe that your mother loved Julian Gatewood, and that he loved her, and you."

Desi cleared her throat. "My mother wouldn't want me putting her business out there like that, Ms. Parker."

"Call me Sue, please," she said, sincerely. "You mother was a private woman?"

"Very."

"Now I see where you get it from. But don't you think that people have tainted her memory long enough?"

"I thought you wanted to write a book about my life. Not my mother's."

"Aren't they intertwined? Ida Green deserved so much better than what she got, Desi. She lost her daughter, her dignity, the man she loved, and eventually her life. You lost your mother, your freedom. Has anyone ever asked you why you did it?"

Desi didn't answer.

"I'm offering you a chance to set the facts straight. You didn't just shoot him for no reason, Desi. Something made you pull that trigger, and the moment you did, the course of your life changed forever.

The Gatewoods are powerful people. The media has always been on their side. They've told their story, and they've made it clear that theirs is the right one, and that yours isn't worth hearing. They pointed fingers at a teenager, and placed the weight of everything that happened on her shoulders. How could you have been responsible for Julian Gatewood's affair with your mother, Desi? And what made you pull that trigger?"

Sue waited again for Desi to say something.

"I'm not asking for an answer right now," Sue continued, calmly. "I'm asking you to just think about it. If you really want to close that chapter of your life, once and for all, just think about it." She paused again. "Desi? Are you there?"

"I'm here," she said, softly.

Sue Parker went on to say that if Desi agreed to do this, she could have the publisher put her contract in the mail. Desi stood on her back patio and lit a cigarette. She'd been trying to quit, but times like this called for a smoke. A pattern was definitely starting to emerge. What the hell was going on? It was like somebody was standing behind her, pushing her towards places she'd have never thought she wanted to go. On the one hand, she had Lonnie with all her conspiracy theories, and vendettas, judges, and now this Sue Parker and her book. In the middle was Desi, wishing she could forget that her whole life had happened. Standing over her was Jordan Gatewood, looking down on top of her ready to pound her on top of the head with his fist.

What would he think if he found out that Desi was having a book published? What would be in that book? How much would she be willing to tell? And would anybody even believe her? Did it matter?

Julian Gatewood, Ida Green, and Desi. For a time, they were the only three people in the world as far as Desi was concerned, and the night he died, people took what they had and turned it into something that never was. The three of them loved each other, and they loved being together, and the only way Desi could've ever made it through prison was by fueling herself on what they had together. They had been so good at taking everything away from her, except her memories. Not even Jordan could touch those. Desi had been afraid for a long time, and she was tired of it. Finally, she was tired.

"Keep your mouth shut, Desi, or else they'll twist your words. They're good at that. And they'll make it sound like you said something you didn't. Let 'em believe their lies. Let 'em tell their lies. Take the truth with you and keep it close to your heart. It'll be safe there."

She'd heeded her mother's advice for more than twenty-five years. Desi's silence had been a sort of homage to Ida Green's memory. But now she was starting to think that maybe her mother wasn't so wise. Maybe Ida was just foolish.

Solomon

His opponent outweighed him by at least fifty pounds, but since when had Solomon ever let a little thing like size stand in his way of a good fight? The big man, Nick, swung a heavy roundhouse which was surprisingly fast, and would've knocked him out of the ring if it had landed. Solomon crouched low, feeling the warm whip of air as it passed over his head. He leaned in close and sucker punched the dude just below the rib.

Hitting his body was like hitting a cement wall, though, and he wondered how much if any affect body blows were having on this giant. He spun low, and sunk deep into his knees, as the big man attempted an uppercut, and missed, when Solomon fell backward on his hands. Using moves from Brazilian martial arts called capoeira, he twisted, turned, and spun around on his hands and feet until he magically appeared behind Nick, sprung up on the balls of his feet, wrapped his arm around Nick's neck, and punched him hard in the kidney.

"Ugh!" his opponent grunted, caving in to the pain.

Solomon smirked, released his grip, and let him stumble off toward one corner of the ring. Yeah. That hurt.

The other fighter managed to spin around, but Solomon was too quick for him. He dropped to his side on the mat and swept a muscular leg out from under Big Nick, catching him by surprise and sending him tumbling to the floor like a giant oak tree, down on his back. Solomon bounced up onto the soles of his bare feet, rushed to the man's head, and stood over him. He grabbed a handful of Nick's hair, drew back his fist, and was just about to deliver what would've been a fatal blow to his Adam's apple, before Carl, the referee and coach, blew the whistle.

Solomon stopped short.

Carl laughed. "You've known Nick too damn long to kill him now, Sol!" he said, holding out water bottles for both men.

Solomon helped Nick to his feet, and patted him on the shoulder as Nick left the ring. "Good job, man."

Nick grunted.

"You sure you don't want to get back in the ring and make some money?" Carl grinned, handing Solomon a towel.

Solomon caught his breath enough to laugh. "I'm too old for this," he said, gasping. "Those young cats would kick my ass."

"Nick didn't."

"That's because he's as old as I am," Solomon retorted. "And fat."

"I heard that!" Nick shouted from the locker room.

After his workout, Solomon quickly showered, dressed, and hurried back to his office in downtown Dallas. He had to fly out later this afternoon for a funeral in Allen, Texas, after a meeting with Desdimona Green.

Solomon Jones was a senior partner in one of the top law firms in the state. He was an entertainment attorney and his client list included the names of professional football and basketball players, musicians, and even a few actors. But when her name came on his schedule, he couldn't help but do a double take. Desdimona Green was as famous in Texas as she was infamous. As soon as he found out about the meeting, Solomon gathered every bit of information he could on the woman.

She was eighteen when she killed Julian Gatewood in her mother's living room. It came out that the old man was having an affair with the mother, and had been for years in a town called Blink, less than a hundred miles northeast of Dallas. Desi shot him, and was sent to prison for the murder. She got out twenty-five years later and inherited a shit-load of his money, which he'd left to her mother in a trust that no one could touch, including the Gatewood heirs, in particular, his wife Olivia and oldest son, Jordan. Apparently, Jordan Gatewood had tried everything in his power to stop the inheritance; he'd spent millions, and lost to Desi's team of lawyers who'd heard about her case all the way over in San Francisco, and took her case on contingency. If she didn't get paid then they didn't get paid, which served as motivation for them to win.

Solomon had only seen grainy, newspaper photos of Desdimona Green on the Internet. He was not prepared for how lovely she was in person. But money could make anybody look good.

Desi walked over to him with her hand extended. "Thank you for agreeing to meet with me, Mr. Jones."

At six-one, Solomon quickly sized her up at five-three, maybe five-four. Like most men, he wouldn't recognize a weave if it bit him on the lip, but weave or not, the thick tresses of silky black hair hanging past her shoulders made him wonder what it would feel like to touch it. Red-framed glasses perched on her nose and framed warm, dark eyes, and a rich wine color stained her lips. Desi wore designer jeans, a pink satin blouse, and low-heeled pumps. If it weren't for the fact that the woman had spent way too much time in prison for murder, he'd have been in love already.

Desi had an elegance to her that contradicted every assumption he'd made about her before she'd stepped into his office. She had an air of privilege that he hadn't expected. Desi Green hadn't been born rich, but she wore it like second skin.

She sat quietly while he flipped through the pages of the contract she'd received from Leviathan Publishing.

"I have to say I'm a bit surprised by your visit, Miss Green," he finally said.

"Why?" she asked, staring at him.

"I would think you'd have your own attorney who could look this contract over for you. Why come to me?"

The publisher had offered her a half-million dollar advance for the publishing rights to her life story.

"I'd heard that you were the best entertainment lawyer in town." The expression on her face suddenly tensed. "Not that anyone should find stories like this entertaining." She glanced away, looking embarrassed.

"Of course not," he agreed.

"Since it's a publishing contract, I just thought you'd be more experienced with things like this."

"They approached you?"

She shrugged. "I was as surprised as you are now."

He'd seen footage of eighteen-year-old Desi Green in handcuffs, being dragged into a courtroom and eventually, off to prison. The girl in that footage had been painfully young, innocent, and scared. The woman sitting across from him now was none of those things.

Despite his best efforts to be objective, Solomon felt uneasy about this. A good lawyer seldom let his personal feelings come between him and his client. But there was something not right about a convicted murderer being paid money like this to write a book. A man was dead because of her. Sure, she'd served time for his death, but she'd also reaped some serious benefits from it too. She'd slapped Julian's family in the face with those benefits—his money—and now she wanted to rub their noses in the mud even more by writing a tell-all book?

"You intend to accept this offer?" he asked, cautiously.

She shrugged. "I wouldn't be here if I didn't." Desi forced a smile.

He studied her lovely face, looking long and deep for even an ounce of hesitation or remorse, but there was none and he was starting to resent her for it.

He knew Jordan Gatewood, if only in passing. They traveled in the same social circles, even had some of the same friends, and were members of the same country club. The man was a successful businessman. He'd taken over his father's business dealings when he was just a kid, and stunned everybody by taking an already successful oil business, refining it, and then turning it into the global empire that it was now. Gatewood had expanded his father's business beyond oil, and had branched off into construction, manufacturing, and even dabbled in some aerospace. To say the man was a mogul was an understatement. He respected him, and for Solomon to facilitate a transaction like this, after what this woman had done to the Gatewood family, felt disrespectful.

Solomon immediately recognized the queasy feeling gnawing at his stomach. It was nausea brought on by a serious lack of moral fortitude. And he'd almost compromised himself for pretty brown eyes and pretty hair.

"Honestly, I don't feel comfortable about this," he said, decidedly. "Maybe I can recommend someone else who can assist you with this matter."

An unexpected flash of disappointment reflected in her eyes. For a moment, she looked like that vulnerable kid again that he'd seen on the internet.

"You were recommended to me. I was told that you were the best in the state."

"I cannot, in good conscience, represent you in this matter," he told her. "It's a pretty straight-forward contract, Miss Green. Any contracts attorney can help you with this."

For a moment, Desi Green looked as if she would break down and cry. But it didn't last long.

"There's always more than one side to a story, Mr. Jones," she said, holding on to her resolve.

"I understand that."

"But you've made it up in your mind that I don't deserve to tell mine?"

"I never said that. I just said that you'll have to get yourself another attorney." He placed the contract back in the envelope and slid it across to Desi. "I can have my assistant provide you with a half dozen names of capable attorneys who would love to sign on to a deal like this."

Desi didn't budge. She just stared at the package in front of her. "I loved him, too," she said, softly. She looked up at Solomon. "My mother loved him," she continued. "And he loved us. The Gatewoods knew, and they hated us for it."

"They were his family, Miss Green," he said, holding her gaze.

Desi swallowed. "And so were we. Everybody thinks they know what happened that night, but the only person who truly knows is me. Everything they have to say about us and Mr. J is wrong, and it's not true," her voice trailed off.

"Who's to say what you have to put in that book is true?" he argued.

"Maybe nobody will buy that book." Desi swallowed. "I don't really care."

"Why do it?"

"I owe it to them, Momma and Mr. J. All anybody thinks is that she was a homewrecker, and he was a cheat who had the misfortune of getting shot for his troubles. There's so much more." Her voice trailed off. "So, much more to him than that."

Solomon couldn't help but to find her argument compelling, and like any good lawyer, he was a sucker for compelling arguments.

"The fact is," he finally said, "this is going to be your word against theirs."

"It's my word." She shrugged. "That's all it is. I just want a chance to say what I have to say."

Solomon paused and thought for a few moments before finally voicing his decision. The longer he listened, the more that sick feeling in his gut began to subside. The woman's whole life had been played out in the media since she was a kid. It only made sense that she should be able to tell her side of it in hardback.

"Can you leave it with me, and let me look it over?" He glanced at his watch. "I have to leave. I have a funeral to attend."

Desi looked hopeful. "Yes," she said, getting up to leave. "That's no problem."

He stood up and walked her out to the reception area. "I can call you in a couple of days."

She nodded. "Thank you," she said appreciatively. "Oh, and I'm sorry for your loss too."

"Thank you."

"Someone close to you?"

"My mother's sister, Mary."

She hesitated for a moment. "I know a woman named Mary who just passed away too. What was her last name?"

"Travis. Mary Travis." He waited for her response. "Same Mary?"

Desi lied. "No. Someone else."

It's Who You Know

Lonnie went into every investigative situation with an open mind, but she always followed her gut. Sometimes her gut was right on, and sometimes it was off a bit, but not by much.

Damn mosquito bites were all over her arms and legs. Served her right for traipsing through Texas backwood country in shorts and a T-shirt. The nasty little critters feasted on her sweet, black ass for a good hour before she fired off her camera for one shot that was worth anything.

Lonnie couldn't believe how hard she had to argue her point, for Desi to let her do this. The woman was too damn afraid of the munchkin from Munchkin land as far as Lonnie was concerned. She'd done her homework. Fleming was sixty-eight, wasn't much taller than Desi, thick around the middle, and balding with a swath of no more than fifty strands of gray hair that grew long enough on one side of his head, to be painstakingly combed over to the other side and glued down with some sort of gel. Lonnie had seen pugs who looked scarier than he did, but still, to an eighteen-year-old girl on trial for murder, a troll like him, who held the fate of your life in his hands, could be pretty frightening. Her girl was starting to come around, though. Desi had told Lonnie about her agreeing to write a book with a *New York Times* bestselling author about her life.

"This is huge, Des." Lonnie was so excited, she almost turned flips. "This is what I'm talking about, girl. Time to do your thing, Des. Stop running, stop hiding, and stand your ground."

"They're not going to be happy when they find out," she said, looking more proud of herself than Lonnie had ever seen her look.

"Fuck their happiness," Lonnie shot back. "They had no problem fucking yours."

A long-range lens could tell stories no one wanted to be told.

"Tsk! Tsk!" she said, shaking her head. Desi's judge was a perv.

One by one, she studied black-and-white photographs of this man's journey into his sin. Each picture told more of the story of his transgression with a lover young enough to have been his grandchild. Lonnie stared at one photo in particular of the man coming out of that windowless building after dark, his tie undone and hanging loose around his neck, his collar unbuttoned. In the next one, she saw his lover, thin, frail, trailing behind him like little kids tended to do, desperate for attention and approval. In another photo, the old man stopped at the driver's side door of his car, gazed deeply into the eyes of his lover, and laughed.

Lonnie's favorite was the last one. It was nearly touching, and if she didn't know better, she'd have truly believed that the two of them were in love. It was the image of the old man, gently cradling his lover's lean, prepubescent face, pressing his lips tenderly against goth-like lips painted black.

Lonnie uploaded the digital images to her computer and studied them closely on the two large flatscreen monitors on her desk in her home office. Lonnie hit the speed-dial telephone button on one of the computer screens and waited for Desi to answer.

"Where are you?" Lonnie asked.

"At the salon."

"I keep telling you to ditch that place. I know a great barber who'll give you a tight-ass buzz cut and get you in and out in less than forty-five minutes," she teased.

"Somedays, girl, I'm tempted."

"Guess what I'm looking at?"

"Is it long, thick, and hard?" Desi joked.

"I wish. No, it's short, round, old, and bald, and nasty, very very nasty."

Desi paused. "Where are you?"

"I'm at home, and I'm looking at pictures of that judge of yours, creeping in the worst way."

"There's only one way to creep, Lon."

"Show's how little you know."

"So, what's in the pictures?"

Lonnie took her time answering. "People pay me a lot of money for what I do, Desi. Do you know why?"

"You want me to pay you?" Desi asked, surprised.

"Not from you. Never from you. I'm just reminding you of how good I am at what I do."

"Damn good."

"You got it."

"So, he's having an affair? We kind of suspected that, though, Lonnie."

"He's having an affair with a pup young enough to be his grand-child. Strike that . . . great-grandchild."

"What?" Desi sounded shocked.

"Baby can't be no more than fifteen, sixteen."

"C'mon, Lonnie. Don't tell me that. Maybe you made a mistake."

"Might be younger than that," Lonnie continued.

"He's a pedophile?" Desi asked in a hushed tone.

"A big one, Des. They're pimping kids out in that place. A bunch of old farts and a few young ones, in and out of that place all day and all night long. It's disgusting."

Desi was speechless.

"I guess we should call the police or something," Desi finally suggested.

"Won't do any good," Lonnie sighed. "The police were in the place. I saw a couple of cop cars parked out back."

"Oh, Lonnie," Desi gasped. "That's . . . oh . . ."

"We can do better than calling the police, Des. We can go to the media, blow that shit wide open."

"I can't believe . . . kids."

"I'll e-mail you the pictures."

"Alright. Yeah. I need to see them."

"See, what did I tell you, Desi. Everybody's got a secret, some worse than others. While he was sitting up on that bench passing judgement on you, he was probably molesting somebody else's child."

"That's a damn shame," Desi said, sadly.

"We're ready for you now, Miss Green." Lonnie heard the salon attendant say to Desi.

"I've got to go, Lonnie."

"I just hit send on those files, Des. They'll be in your inbox when you get home."

Desi hung up without saying good-bye.

"Let he who is without sin . . ." She murmured at the irony. He had made his living judging other people. But wasn't that always the way? Dirty bastards ran the world, doing whatever the hell they wanted to do, under the guise of privilege. He'd screwed one child and sent her to prison, probably sitting on that bench trying to figure out how to screw another one and he deserved whatever came of this.

Stormy Weather

Jordan was tall like his father, but he wasn't as light as Mr. J had been, and he didn't have blue eyes. He looked more like his mother and he looked like he'd been born in a stack of money, wearing it with the same flair that he wore that expensive tailored suit, and silk tie.

"This bitch kills him and then gets his money? Somebody wake me the hell up from this nightmare!"

"Counselor," the judge sitting at the end of the conference table said, sternly. "Please remind your client that that sort of behavior will not be tolerated in my court."

She was fresh out of prison. Desi didn't like judges, or lawyers because at any moment she felt like any one of them could've thrown her ass back in prison if she so much as sneezed. And Jordan Gatewood scared the hell out of Desi. The last time she'd seen him in person, he was young, just a few years older than she was, sitting behind her in that courtroom behind the prosecutor, glaring at her with laser eyes. Even then she didn't have the courage to look at him. She couldn't bring herself to look at him now.

Ida's will had said that she'd left Desi all her belongings, including the house, and money that Desi didn't know her mother had. No one knew she had that kind of money, not even the Gatewoods. Apparently, Mr. J had been sneaky in leaving it to her, figuring out some way to keep it secret. Jordan Gatewood didn't find out about it until word got out that Desi had inherited millions. He got suspicious, set his attorneys loose on her, and found out that the only way Desi could've inherited that kind of money was if Julian had left it to her.

"She's benefitting from the death of the very man she killed, your honor!" Jordan blurted out, ignoring his lawyer's pleading that he keep quiet. "For all I know, she killed him to get the money. Maybe there's your motive for murder right there! You killed my father because you knew he'd left millions to you!"

Desi leaned over to her lawyer and whispered. "I inherited my momma's money."

Jordan overheard her. He pounded his fist so hard on that conference table that Desi thought it would break in two. She jumped in her seat when he stood up, looking like he wanted to leap over that table, wrap his hands around her neck, and squeeze until he snapped it.

"That whore got that money from my father!"

Red flashed behind her eyes, and in a blur, Desi stood up, and hurled her purse across the table right at him. "Don't you talk about my momma like that!" she yelled.

He swatted the purse like it was a fly.

"That's it! That's enough!" The judge stood up and yelled. "Get these people out of my court! Get them out of here, now!"

In the end, she'd won. There wasn't a person in that room who thought she'd had a snowball's chance in hell of getting that money, least of all, him. A man like that wasn't used to losing to anybody. And the fact that he'd lost to her, ate him up inside.

Desi inhaled her cigarette. She stood in the middle of her empty living room, tapping the ashes into an soda can.

"What the hell is my problem?" she murmured to herself. She'd been living in this place like a visitor who could be told to leave at any minute. This was her home. It was shiny and brand new and it was hers. When was it going to finally sink in that she deserved a house like this? When was she going to accept the turn that her life had taken? After all, she'd earned it. She'd paid with her life for this place. Her mother had paid for it with her life. And Mr. J? He'd wanted Desi and Ida to have that money. He'd gone to such great lengths to hide it from his family and fancy lawyers, because he didn't want anybody else to take it from them, because he loved them. He loved them as much as they had loved him. And maybe in some way, he had loved them more than he'd loved his real family.

They were all liars. Even Ida Green had been a liar, by not telling Desi the truth about the man she loved.

"Is Mr. J your husband?" a very young Desi asked her mother once.

Ida smiled. "He is my husband here." She placed her hand over her heart.

Desi thought about it, and then asked the only other question she could ask. "Is he my daddy in my heart?"

Ida's smile faded. "He's your daddy all over, Desi."

And he was.

Desi needed to finally put down some roots in this place. She began picturing in her mind the kind of furnishings she wanted in this room, and the way she wanted it to make her feel when she walked in. She'd only bought this big-house because she could afford it, and rich people lived in big houses. More than the house, it was the land she loved. Desi owned three thousand glorious acres of open space. She didn't have another neighbor in sight, and even owned her own private road.

She'd spent more than half of her life living in a box, a six-by-six-foot cell. Now she lived in a castle, one that was way too big, but maybe she could find a way to make it fit.

It was time to make alot of things fit and not just the house, but the money, too. It was time to make the truth fit, all of it, especially the parts she'd ignored all these years and pretended like none of it ever happened. When Mr. J was alive, he'd taken care of Desi and her mother, and he'd made sure to take care of them after he'd died, too. That money Desi had inherited was rightfully hers, and not even Jordan Gatewood, with all his power, money, and attorneys, could take it from her.

She closed her eyes, took a deep breath, and visualized two words, while saying them out loud. "You won. You won. You won."

The Man

"Dad, I need my car keys."

Solomon Jones closed the refrigerator, leaned back against the kitchen counter, and casually twisted off the cap on his beer bottle.

Her car keys?

He finished half the bottle before finally coming up for air, releasing a room-shaking burp and looking at her like she'd lost her mind.

Right on cue came the eye-rolling, the folding of the arms across the chest, and the lip smacking. If he wanted to, he could write a thesis about a teenage girl and be right on the money.

"Daddyyyyyyy." Sonya whined, dropped her arms, and stomped one flip-flopped foot, just like he knew she would. "You said I could have them back todayyyyyyy."

"Did I?" he asked, indifferently.

When she was younger, and cuter, he'd fall for that shit every single time. But now she was a teenager. He hated teenagers, even his own, especially when she stood in his kitchen looking more like her mother, who'd decided after summer break was over and it was time to fly this child back to Chicago to go to school, that maybe it would be a good idea for her to go to school, that nice private one, in Texas so that she could spend more time with her father.

"You diiiiiiiid." Poke out bottom lip. Drop chin to chest. Bat pretty brown eyes, and stomp over to *Daddy* the way she used to do when she was five. Hold out her hand, like she knows *Daddy's* going to break down and give in to her little tantrum. Pout. "Please Daddy?"

Be strong, man. Don't give in to that—Get your hand out of your pocket! Solomon! Man!

Big grin. "Thank you, Daddy." Quick peck on the cheek, spin around and race out of the house before he comes to his senses and changes his mind.

"Be back by eight!" he shouted after her.

"Nine?"

"Eight thirty or I'm coming after you!"

"'Kay!"

Solomon and his wife, Tracy, had only been married for three years before the thrill of the sex wore off, the kid came, and they realized that they couldn't stand being married to each other. A few years later, she remarried, move to Chi-town, and had a set of twin boys to keep her busy. Solomon counted his blessings. Those twins could've just as easily been his. Sonya was his baby girl and she was more than enough. She'd said she wanted to go away to college. Her mother was against it. He wasn't.

Solomon had just sat down and turned on the Cowboy's game when his phone rang. It was Mark Evans, a friend of his from the country club.

"So, I'm playing the seventh hole on the green when a friend of mine asks about you, some publishing contract, and a murderer. I stood there looking stupid, waiting for the punch line."

Of course Solomon wasn't surprised. If you wanted to keep something on the low in this city, all you had to do was not tell anybody about it.

"And you're calling me, because—"

"Because Jordan Gatewood was playing in front of me on the eighth hole. Some dude in a suit and tie crossed the green to get to him, said something to the man, and the next thing I know, his nine iron goes sailing through the air and whizzing past my head. And then, although I could be wrong, I could've sworn I heard your name come up among quite a few choice profanities. But like I said, maybe I heard wrong."

Solomon was used to people talking about him at the club. After all, he did represent some of the biggest names in the entertainment and professional sports industries. Somehow, though, he just knew that this was not going to be good.

"You going to tell me what's going on?" Mark asked.

"I'd so much rather get back to this game I was just about to watch."

"I see. Going into button-lip mode on me, huh?"

Solomon chuckled. "Like it matters, I mean, you're calling me from the golf course telling me about it."

"The only killer I know that could draw that kind of reaction from Gatewood is the infamous Miss Green," Mark concluded.

Solomon took another gulp of his beer. "That's the only one I know of too."

"She was in your office less than a week ago?"

"You called Katy on a Sunday to ask her that?" Katy was Solomon's administrative assistant.

"She and I go way back," he said sarcastically.

"And she told you that Desi Green was in my office?"

If she had, then come Monday morning her ass was out of a job.

"No, she didn't. She said she couldn't comment on it one way or another and asked if in the future I'd refrain from calling her at home on the weekends."

Good for her!

"Then how'd you know she was in my office?"

He laughed. "I didn't, until now. Damn! I'm glad you're not my attorney."

Solomon couldn't believe he'd fallen for that shit. "Fuck you, man," he said, dismally.

"What'd she want?"

"None of your damn business."

"That's fine. You don't have to tell me. I'm not going to take it personally."

"You should."

"I just called to tell you to be on your guard, man. And expect a phone call at the office on Monday, maybe even a visit. I have a feeling that Gatewood is planning on getting to know you a whole lot better than just in passing on the golf course."

Solomon sighed. "I'll be sure to heed the warning, man."

"That's all I ask. Go Green Bay!" Green Bay was playing Dallas.

"Go sit on your putter, man. Hard."

He hung up the phone, watched Romo toss the ball twenty yards down the field to Miles, who dropped it. But his mind wasn't on the game anymore. Without even trying he'd been pulled into the middle of World War Three, the endless battle between Desi Green and Jordan Gatewood. He'd seen it coming, though. The minute she walked into his office, and he agreed to be her attorney for this business transaction, he'd seen it coming.

The last thing he needed was controversy. Jordan was famous for shooting attorneys out of cannons at people who didn't get with the program, his program. The way he saw it, Solomon could avoid all this nonsense by giving Desi back her contract and washing his hands of the matter, but then, that would be a punk move, and just like Green Bay was owning the Cowboys, Gatewood would own him.

Treasure Box

The old woman had special treasures that she kept in a box hidden in a compartment in her closet. Olivia wore the key on a gold chain around her neck.

She pulled a gold ring out of the box with a diamond so small, she had to squint to see it. Olivia laughed to herself. It was her first promise ring. She was just a girl when that young man gave it to her. Olivia pulled a neatly folded baby blue, linen handkerchief from the box next. "Something borrowed—something blue," she murmured, fingering the royal blue embroidered lettering in one corner, OF, Olivia Franklin. Franklin had been her maiden name. On the opposite corner were the letters OG, Olivia Gatewood. Her mother had given this to her minutes before her wedding. She searched the box for another valuable item she'd held dear, and kept close. Olivia rummaged through it, pulling everything out and laying it neatly on the bed. "Where is it?" she asked, confused, sliding the contents that she'd placed on the bed all around, hoping to come across it, but instead, she came across something else.

It was an old section from the newspaper, folded and faded.

MILLIONAIRE JULIAN GATEWOOD MURDERED!

She didn't bother unfolding it. Olivia had read through it a hundred times, and she knew what it said. "Shh, Olivia," she said to herself. What they wrote—the papers—

She had kept every article ever written about Desi Green. Olivia's memory wasn't always clear or accurate. But the one thing she could never do was forget that child's face. Olivia had never stopped hating her.

She looked so much like her mother, Ida. Olivia wondered how many of Julian's business trips had been spent in that house, with Ida and that little girl? A wife has her suspicions. Something deep inside her warns her when her man is being unfaithful. Several years into their marriage, Olivia began to have her suspicions and late one night, after he'd come home from being gone most of the week, she confronted him with them.

Olivia's babies were both asleep in their rooms down the hall. "You think I'm a fool?" she asked, exasperated. "You think I don't know?"

Julian kept unpacking his bag, while Olivia stood over him, and followed him around the room, trying to corner him, to make him stop and look her in the eyes.

"Who is she, Julian?" Olivia sobbed. "And don't tell me I'm overreacting, because I know I'm not!"

She grabbed him by the arm, and Julian dropped a handful of shirts on the floor. She'd never forget the look on his face, in his eyes.

"It's none of your goddamned business, Olivia," he said, gritting his teeth and jerking away from her.

She couldn't believe he'd said that to her. Wasn't she his wife? Wasn't she the mother of his children? "It—it is my business," she said, shocked that he'd had the nerve to suggest that it wasn't. "I'm your wife. Julian! I'm your wife! It is my business!"

"Leave it alone," he muttered, picking up his shirts and taking them into the closet.

Olivia was confused. She was angry, and she hadn't expected his reaction. She'd expected him to lie, to tell her that she was worried over nothing. She'd expected him to tell her she was imagining things. She'd expected him to fight to try and keep her, and to keep their marriage together.

"I won't live like this," she finally said. "Julian, I don't have to live like this!"

She stood up and stalked over to him again.

"Then don't!" He looked into her eyes as he said it.

Stunned, she stumbled backward. "I'll take the children."

A muscle in his jaw ticked. "You do what you have to."

Was he choosing her over Olivia? Was he really doing that? "Julian?"

He didn't say a word. Julian's crystal blue eyes locked onto hers, daring her to follow through with her threat. She never did.

When he was alive, Julian had not been a nice man. He wasn't even a decent man, but Olivia had loved him anyway, even though he did what he wanted without giving any consideration to how the things he did might have affected her. Jordan was just like him. She'd seen Julian's ways in him, in the way he treated his wife and in the way he ignored his daughter, making up for his shortcomings with money.

"Do you love her?" Olivia confronted Julian after finding out about Ida Green. "Do you love her more than me, Julian? More than your children?"

Tears streamed down her cheeks as she begged him to say it, to tell her the truth that had been breaking her heart ever since she found out about his affair with that woman. "Answer me, Julian!"

Julian pushed passed her without saying a word, and left not only their bedroom that night, but their house.

Desi Green was all that was left of Ida. And Desi Green, it seemed, would live forever, a constant reminder of everything she had loved and lost, her husband, her dignity, her salvation.

"I can't pray enough." Mary Travis had been such a quiet woman. She'd recently passed away, but shortly before that, she'd called Olivia.

"Why are you calling me?"

Olivia knew of Mary Travis. She was the forewoman presiding over Desi's trial.

"Because I had to hear your voice," she said, her voice raspy and weak. "We've never said two words to each other."

"Why would we?" Olivia asked, annoyed. This woman had no business calling her. The two of them had nothing to talk about.

"Because we made a mistake, Olivia," she said dismally. "We were wrong."

Women like Mary Travis didn't travel in Olivia's social circle. And the woman certainly wasn't familiar enough with her to call her by her given name.

"You are entitled to your opinion, Mrs. Travis," Olivia said smugly. "But what's done is done," she said, nearly choking on that statement. What was done still lingered in the air like a foul odor, even after all these years. "None of us can change the past. I can't bring my husband back, and you can't have back whatever it is you lost."

"My soul?"

"That's between you and God."

"God?" Mary Travis repeated appalled. "God turned his back on me a long time ago. He turned his back on all of us. He doesn't hear us. He doesn't see us. We're dead to him."

Olivia rolled her eyes at the dismal melodrama spewing from that woman's mouth. "Us? There is no *us*, Mary Travis! I don't know you and you don't know me! We had an agreement," Olivia continued. "I kept my part of the bargain and you kept yours."

"We were wrong," Mary sobbed.

"Then you worry about your own salvation, and leave mine the hell alone!" Olivia slammed the phone down before that woman could say another word. One of her attorneys told her about the woman's death a few days later.

"Mary Travis had been confined to a wheelchair. For some reason, according to the coroner, she must've tried to stand and fell and hit her head on the side of the coffee table," he explained. "A neighbor found her a day later. She was dead."

"God turned his back on me . . . on us." Mary's words came back to Olivia's memory.

She didn't expect to take the news of that woman's death so hard. But Olivia found herself crying after hearing about her passing. Only, she wasn't crying for Mary. She cried for all of them.

This Song Is About You

Jordan had been sitting in his Bentley for nearly an hour before Desi finally pulled up into her driveway. She sat in her car for several minutes before finally getting out and walking up the pathway toward her front door, carrying armfuls of shopping bags. Obviously, she was making good use of his father's money. She glanced quickly in his direction when he climbed out of his car and walked toward her.

"Leave me alone, Jordan!" she snapped, letting herself inside.

She'd said his name out loud. He had never heard her say his name before. Somewhere along the line she'd found herself some courage. He had to take his hat off to her for that.

She tried closing the door behind her, but Jordan pushed his way inside. Desi dropped her bags where she stood.

"Get the fuck out of my house!" she shouted, pointing at the door behind him.

"Money buy you some guts, Desi?" he asked, bitingly, stuffing his hands casually into his pockets.

"I want you out of my house!"

Jordan had never hit a woman in his life, but then, this one here wasn't a woman. She was the shit he stepped in on his ranch that he scraped off the bottom of his shoe before he went into the house. As enticing as the idea was to slap the hell out of her, the last thing he wanted to do was dirty his hands with this bitch.

"You don't want to write that book, Desi," he said, taking a step closer to her.

Desi matched it and took a step back.

She clenched her jaws, and put on her best rendition of brave. "And you don't want to try and tell me what to do, Jordan."

He shrugged. "I don't get it. You took the man's life, his money, blood money, and now you want to smear what's left of his reputation?"

"Don't you mean *your* reputation?"

"My reputation is not at stake here," he explained, glaring at her. "Unless you know something I don't," Jordan said, sarcastically. Never in a million years would he ever mistake Desi for a genius, but the thought did cross his mind, briefly, that she could be the one behind those texts and e-mails he had been receiving.

"This has nothing to do with you!" she shouted. "What I do with my life has nothing to do with you!"

Just listening to her, he concluded that Desi Green was an idiot. Nobody that dumb could be capable of tripping up one of the best IT techs in the business. Jordan stepped toward her again. "I feel like I'm on an episode of *Punk'd* or something, as if at any moment some comedian is going to jump out of a closet with a film crew, laughing and telling me that this is all one big crazy gag.

"Just go," she started to cry.

He looked at her, disgusted. "What the hell did that old man see in y'all's ignorant, country asses?"

"Get the hell outta my house!"

"That bitch's pussy must've dripped honey."

She lunged at him this time. "Mother fuck—" Desi swung.

Jordan caught her arm in the air by the wrist, and twisted her arm until she dropped to the floor on her knees.

"Stop it!" she cried. "Let me go." She cringed.

"Don't you ever raise your hand to me!" he growled. "I could break this shit clean off and not give it a second thought?" He twisted it again, one more time before he finally did let go. Jordan pushed her sending her falling backward onto the floor.

He squatted down in front of her and looked her square in the eyes. "All I care about is my family. And the last thing I want is for them to have to go through the humiliation, again, of having their lives played out in the media, for the whole goddamned world to see."

Desi clutched her wrist and sobbed.

"They don't need your lies, Desi. Or whatever bullshit you plan on making up to try and redeem yourself."

"I don't have to lie," she said, threatening. "I know what happened the night he died!"

"Of course you do." He shrugged. "You shot him. You pulled the trigger and shot my father. A convicted killer's version of the truth." He laughed. "Shit, maybe I should just leave you alone and let you write this book of yours."

A jury had convicted her the last time. Maybe this time, Desi would convict herself. Jordan stood up and decided to leave. If anybody was crazy enough to pay money for that damn book, he could

88 / **J. D. Mason**

always sue her for libel and take whatever money she did make from it.

"Sounds like the only fool to come out of all of this will be you."

"Is that what you think?"

He studied her for a moment as she managed to get to her feet. She had cleaned up well. But then, money did that to people, made them look so much better when deep down, they were garbage.

Jordan was finished. "You go ahead and write your book, Desi, and when it's finished, I'll sue you for slander and take every dime you have." He smiled as he turned to leave. "See you back in court."

Desi stumbled over to one of the walls in her living room after he left, braced herself against it, and slid down to the floor. Her heart was racing, and her wrist throbbed from where he'd grabbed it. Jordan Gatewood believed he ruled the world and he believed he could rule her too.

It had taken everything inside her not to blurt out the things she'd planned on telling Sue Parker to put in that book. If he wanted to believe she was just writing it to try and get even, then let him. As long as he believed she was angry and dumb, then that was fine. If she had told him the truth as she planned to tell it, he'd have killed her. And being Jordan Gatewood, he would've gotten away with it.

A Dirty Tale

A Dirty Tale

Confess with My Mouth

"*I had hoped* that everything would turn out alright."

"Everything didn't turn out alright."

"We begged him to take the death penalty off the table. You know how the judges are here in Texas, tossing it around like it's a baseball. I've always believed that they were too careless with death, doling it out as punishment."

"So, the fact that you talked him out of the death sentence, you think that made what you did—what all of you did—alright?"

"I didn't say that."

"Good. Because it doesn't."

"I should've died a long time ago, but the only thing that kept me going was waiting for this day to come. I needed to know and see with my own eyes that that teenage girl survived prison."

"Most people can make it through if they're strong and determined enough."

"But some can't because they're not so strong and they're certainly not prepared."

"I don't think anybody is ever prepared for prison, Mrs. Travis."

"Please. Call me Mary. And you're right, of course. How could anybody be prepared for something so dreadful?"

"But you all decided that fate for someone. You did it for money. You sold the life of another human being that wasn't yours to sell and you did it without giving it a second thought, without blinking."

"Oh, we blinked. And the sinful nature of what we did poisoned each and every one of us, killing us slowly through the years. For every day of that sentence, we all suffered."

"Not enough, Mary. And the Gatewoods didn't suffer either."

"You're right on both counts. Despite what they wanted the rest of the world to believe, the Gatewoods never truly did get what they deserved. I don't think that they even suffered the loss of Julian. For all their crying and tears, I never believed that they felt the loss of that man."

"The money meant nothing to them?"

"It was a drop in the bucket to them, and was more than any one of us would, under any other circumstances, ever see in our lifetime. Back then it was worth it," Mary admitted, shamefully. "People like them buy and sell other people all the time. I'd never seen so much money. I never dreamed that I ever would. I promised myself that I would use it to help people. It kept me from admitting to myself that I was hurting someone else to do it."

"You helped others to clear your conscience?"

Mary nodded. "For a time, it worked. It worked fine. But not forever."

Pretty Things

The pretty one he held in his arms was thin, delicate, and fair with shoulder-length, wavy brown hair, full feather-soft rose-colored lips, moist and ripe for kissing. He closed his eyes and swayed slowly, back and forth to the music, taking great care not to be too rough or too clumsy.

Dancing had never come easily for him. More times than he cared to remember, his wife would limp off the dance floor, cringing after they'd finished dancing, with him trailing pitifully behind her, apologizing profusely for putting her through such torture. She'd always laugh, pat his hand, and smile. "It's alright, honey. You're good at too many other things for me to hold your bad dancing against you."

God! He loved her. He loved her more now than he did when they were first married.

"I'm thirsty," the sweet, young thing in his arms whispered in his ear.

He didn't want to let go, though. Not until the song was finished.

"I'll get you something to drink, sweetheart," he whispered back, "after we finish this dance."

A man in his position was convicted by his transgressions every day, but it was nights like this that forced those guilty and weighing thoughts from his head. Nights like this he could forget his obligations and focus all of his energy on the intense pleasure he felt right now, in this precious moment.

The world was riddled with good and evil, right and wrong, joy and sadness. And his life was a lie. He spent his days and most of his nights pretending to be someone he wasn't, denying himself the pleasures he craved most. Good ol' boys like him didn't entertain the thoughts he had. A real man wouldn't dare do the kinds of things he did, and love them. Most of the time, he felt like he was suffocating, but he had to smile through it, laugh, and throw back a few beers. Coming here was a release from all that. Coming here, he felt like a free man, a world away from the burdens of his life and responsibilities.

This place had no name, just like none of the men who came here had names. It was called a number, 6C825, and it was just a small part of a larger network, just like it. He had VIP access, which he paid dearly for, but it was worth every single dime. There were doctors here, and lawyers, members of the clergy, even congressmen, all of them, men who served their fellow men and women one way or another, giving of themselves sometimes, at the expense of themselves. They came here to get instead of give, to be taken care of and pampered without guilt or shame, or regret.

He stopped dancing and held the long, slender, delicate hands in his, and then gazed longingly into beautiful brown eyes that set him on fire down in his groin. "Let's go and get that drink now," he said, raising the perfect hands to his lips and kissing them one at a time.

Another club member walked over to them, stopped, and stared approvingly at the lovely thing clinging close to him. "You sharing tonight?" he asked.

"Not tonight," he answered, watching the beauty sashay over to the bar and lean seductively over the counter.

The other man smiled and tipped his Stetson. "Shame," he said in that rich, Texas twang.

The pretty one at the bar looked seductively over a slender shoulder back at him, and smiled. No. It wasn't a shame. There was nothing shameful about the flutter he felt in his stomach, anticipating the rest of the evening. He would take his time with this one, and savor every second of their encounter.

Judge Russ Fleming walked over to the young man just as he was getting his drink from the bartender. The sweet, young thing couldn't have been more than seventeen, maybe eighteen. That's what he told himself. That's what he needed to believe.

"Let's take it upstairs, sweetheart," he said, putting his hand low on the young man's waist. Russ guided him toward their destination.

Never Judge a Book

Solomon had been warned to expect a call from Jordan Gatewood, but it didn't come from him. It came to the head of the law firm where Solomon worked.

Xavier Duncan was a relic. He occupied a huge office with picturesque views, walls lined with plaques, awards, degrees, and newspaper articles covering the cases he'd won on behalf of huge corporations. He was a symbol of more than an attorney these days, sitting behind his desk looking every bit as regal and stately as his reputation dictated.

"Sit down, Solomon." He motioned to the chairs in front of his desk.

Xavier was seventy-five, with a head full of thick, silver hair, reddish-brown skin, wearing an expensive European-influenced suit. In the last year, this was only the second time Solomon had set foot in this man's office.

"Tell me about Desdimona Green," he said, directly.

Solomon was caught a bit off guard that the man would mention her name. That's when it dawned on him why he had been summoned to Duncan's office.

"She's a client of mine," Solomon responded casually.

Xavier was never one to beat around the bush and it quickly became obvious that today was not the day for him to break old habits. "Why?"

"She asked me to review a contract for her. I agreed."

"Why?"

The challenge was on the table. Money talked. Bullshit walked. Obviously, Jordan Gatewood had decided to use his influence and change the course of things as he saw fit. And he was using Xavier to do it.

"Because she asked me to."

Soulless gray eyes stared back at him. "It's an uncomfortable situation to be in," Xavier explained.

"Not for me." Solomon shrugged.

Xavier smiled, revealing rows of the most perfect, whitest teeth Solomon had ever seen. "For me."

"I don't understand," he lied. Of course he understood. Gatewood was pissed about the book Desi was going to write. Solomon understood his reasons, but he'd been retained by Desi for this project. Sitting here now, he realized that he'd made a mistake by signing on to do it. It wasn't going to net him a lot of money; not enough to matter in the grand scheme of things. It was a small project in comparison to others he was working on. In truth, it was a waste of his time and energy.

"You could tell her that you are no longer interested in pursuing this endeavor," he said, suggestively.

Solomon nodded. "I could, but it's done. The contract is signed and in the mail on its way back to the publishing house, Xavier."

Xavier sighed, intertwined his fingers together, and leaned forward on his desk. "There are some relationships that are worth cultivating,

Solomon. And some that are not. The success of this firm has been based, in part, on cultivating the ones that prove to be the most beneficial for the firm. Others are simply a waste and not worth the effort."

Solomon nodded. "Okay, so what are you telling me?"

He leaned back. "To pick and choose your battles more wisely, Solomon. We need no part of this one."

"Desi didn't come in here asking for an army to fight any battles. She wanted me to look over a contract."

Was this man serious? Xavier was threatening him with double-talk instead of just coming out and saying what he meant.

"And by accepting, you've managed to put me and this firm in a precarious situation."

"What's precarious about it?"

Solomon hadn't just passed the bar exam. He wasn't an idiot. Xavier recruited him, handpicked him to work at this firm, and now he was treating him like some trained monkey who didn't have a brain.

"I'm asking you to cut her loose," he said, strongly. "It's just a contract. Not a big deal, and certainly not worth the time of an attorney of your caliber."

"You surprise me, Xavier. Never, in all my years at this firm have I ever known you to interfere in another attorney's relationship with a client."

"I never have, until now."

Solomon shook his head. "Gatewood money pressing down on you?" he asked sarcastically.

Xavier didn't respond.

Solomon stood up to leave. "I can appreciate the pressure you must be under, Xavier. Truly. But I'm a big boy, and a damn good attorney, more than capable of handling my workload and choosing my clients and making this firm a great deal of money. If the man has a problem with me, then he needs to come to me. If you have a problem with me, just say the word and I'll pack up my client list and leave. But I'll be damned if you or anybody else is going to tell me how to do my job."

Solomon left, fuming. If Gatewood or even Xavier thought he was some punk that they could push around, then both of them could kiss his ass.

An hour later, Solomon was standing on Desi's doorstep ringing her bell with her negotiated contract in his hand. He'd lied to Xavier about it being sent off to the publisher.

"Hey." She answered the door smiling and barefoot.

Desi wore a simple sundress. Her hair was pulled away from her face. The woman was in her forties, old but in that moment, looked twenty years younger.

"Come on in." She stepped aside. Solomon followed her into a massive but empty living room. The only thing in it was a blanket spread out in the middle of the floor. "The new furniture is being delivered in a few days," she explained sounding a little embarrassed, seeing him standing there looking a bit confused.

"You just move in?"

She nodded. "A while ago."

And she still hadn't bought furniture?

"Is that the contract?"

Desi was prettier than he remembered, compact, with soft curves.

He handed her the package and then followed her into the kitchen to the center island. She looked at him and smiled hesitantly as she opened the envelope and laid out the contract. At first, she just looked at it, and then she began to leaf through each of the pages.

"There's so much here," she said nervously, tentatively glancing up at him. "It's all good though?"

He nodded. "It is now."

In that moment he understood that it wasn't the money that had motivated him to take this project. Solomon, quite frankly, was intrigued. Desi intrigued him. When she first came to his office he expected to meet Desi Green, the bad guy. But that's not what he saw then, and it certainly wasn't what he saw in her now.

"So, I can sign it?" she asked, reluctantly, with beautiful, doe-like eyes.

"Yes," he said, handing her a pen. "And when you're done, I'll drop it in the mail for you."

Camelot

Olivia Gatewood sat up straight in her chair and gasped softly at the sight of him walking through the door. Oh, what a fine man he was. Tall, café au lait brown, with hooded eyes and a goatee perfectly trimmed framing perfect lips and a strong, square chin. She demurely averted her gaze and privately scolded herself for being so forward and so brazen as to stare, but . . . She slowly raised her gaze to meet his. He was staring too. Of course he was, she blushed. Olivia was a beautiful woman, and men stared. They couldn't help themselves.

Jordan stopped before approaching his mother sitting on the patio just outside her bedroom suite. "How is she today, Abby?" he whispered to Olivia's private nurse.

"Today's a good day," she whispered back. "But she may not know you," she gently warned.

Jordan thanked her and walked over to his mother. She wouldn't look at him, but he could tell that she was acting out a role she was used to playing. Olivia was a beautiful, Southern woman, reserved but flirtatious. There had been a time in her life when men had flocked to her, bearing gifts and promises, courting her the way a lady of her caliber should be courted, hoping to be the one she chose.

"Good afternoon," he said, smiling. Jordan had been the object of this game before with his mother, and he didn't mind indulging her from time to time. To refer to her as mother, or to remind her now, of such a thing, when she was that younger version of herself in her mind, would've been cruel.

She delicately cleared her throat, folded her small hands in her lap, and avoided looking at him. "Good evening," she said in a tone as delicate as flower petals.

Olivia's health began deteriorating after Julian's death. The stress of the trial and the public attention weighed heavily on her. Olivia had a series of mini strokes, until a major one nearly took her life. Dementia had set in nearly a decade ago, and Jordan and his sister Janelle, who now lived in Atlanta, watched painfully as their mother vanished inside a shell of her former self.

Before Julian's death, Olivia had been one of the most intriguing socialites in Texas, but as time went on, she retreated to the thirty-five-thousand-acre Gatewood estate north of Dallas, and became a recluse. Olivia seldom left the house anymore.

Miss Black Texas, 1961, Olivia Franklin was a sight to behold back then. His mother was the love of his life. She was seventy, and despite the deep lines etched around her eyes and mouth, the silver streaking through her hair, the crooked angle of her mouth when she smiled, she was still the most beautiful woman he'd ever laid eyes on.

"May I offer you something cool to drink?" Olivia asked politely.

He smiled. His mother's eyelashes fluttered and she hesitantly smiled back.

"Yes. Thank you," Jordan replied.

She waved her hand in the air to get the nurse's attention.

"Yes, ma'am?" Abby responded promptly and in character. She looked at Jordan, and winked so that Olivia wouldn't see her.

"Could you please bring us two glasses of iced tea?" She looked at Jordan. "With lemon?"

He nodded.

"With lemon," she continued.

"Certainly," the nurse said, smiling, before disappearing.

"I hope you can stay for supper," Olivia said coyly, brushing a stray hair from her face.

"It would be my pleasure, Miss Franklin," Jordan told her.

He'd never been particularly close to his father. There were times when Julian was as much an anomaly to Jordan as he was to any stranger on the street. Most of the time, Julian seemed to wish he were someplace else on those rare occasions when he was home. He was tolerant of his wife. Olivia pretended not to notice. His sister pretended not to care. Jordan stayed away from him. When he found out his father was dead, it wasn't Julian that he mourned. It was Olivia. He watched her heart break and a part of her died with him.

Desi was supposed to just go away. She was supposed to take the money and disappear from their lives. He'd spent millions on sorry-ass attorneys who couldn't stop the inheritance. Desi had occupied every single day of his life for the last twenty-six years. Her name was always in the back of his mind, on the tip of his tongue.

Olivia was fragile, and she'd been hurt so much by the man she loved, the man who was supposed to love and cherish her. She'd been humiliated to the point that she'd become a hermit in that house. Desi was crazy if she believed he'd let her put his mother through that embarrassment all over again. The bitch didn't have to say it but he knew what she planned on putting in that book. He had decided to wait, and let her make a fool of herself. Nobody in their right mind would believe her lies. It was her word against theirs. But if even one person believed her story, it would be one person too many.

"There's a simple fix to this problem, Jordan. All this can be over, and you and your family can get on with your lives, put this behind you."

"What do you need from me?"

Jordan was just a kid, not much older than Desi, but he was his father's voice now.

"Permission."

The team of lawyers never told him the details, and he didn't ask. Desi Green was found guilty. That's all that mattered.

"We're having a lovely roasted quail tonight for supper," his mother said eloquently. "With sweet peas, and a fresh tossed salad. For dessert," she smiled coyly, "I've made peach cobbler from scratch. You do like peach cobbler. Don't you?"

He smiled. "Yes. I love peach cobbler."

Olivia blushed.

Judge Not

Russ Fleming had been retired for six years, and he'd all but forgotten that that girl had even existed until he read in the paper that she had inherited millions from Julian Gatewood. Justice certainly had a sense of humor. She had been convicted of killing a man, and then ended up with his money. Russ was old enough to be able to tout that he'd seen it all, but that right there caused him to stumble a bit.

"Desdimona Green's writing a book." Tom Billings called out of the blue. Like Russ, he'd retired years ago, and the two of them hadn't spoken in ages. "It's in the paper," Tom explained with his slow way of talking.

"I know." Russ sighed. "I've read about it."

Neither of them said a word for several minutes. Both men were in their late sixties, and had grown up together in Blink. Tom was the sheriff twenty-six years ago when Desi Green was arrested for murder. Russ ended up being the judge presiding over the case. A big thing like murder in a small town like Blink was news enough, but a big thing like the murder of one of the richest men in Texas was almost too much for their small town to handle.

A tidal wave of reporters rushed Blink from all over the country to cover the story of the teenage girl who'd shot and killed Gatewood. Desi Green was eighteen at the time, but she could've passed for twelve or thirteen.

"What do you think she's going to write about?" Tom probed.

"Her life, Tom," Russ shot back. "It says she's writing a book about her life. I take it that's what it'll be about."

Again, Tom hesitated. Russ could almost hear the wheels turning in the man's head through the phone.

"What are you worried about, Tom?" Russ asked, irritably.

His wife came out onto the porch carrying two glasses of lemonade. She put one down on the small table close to him, and kissed his cheek. She sat down in the chair next to him, and sipped from her glass.

"I ain't worried," Tom finally said.

"Good."

"But . . ."

Russ sighed, frustrated. "But what?"

"I saw her a few weeks ago," Tom explained. "You know that she sold the house."

"I heard."

"I don't know, Russ. Now that she's got all that money . . . I don't think it's right for her to go off and write a book. She needs to let the past stay in the past and let the Gatewoods rest in peace."

"There's no law against writing a book, Tom, and even if there was, there wouldn't be a damn thing you or I could do about it."

Tom was quiet for several beats before continuing. "You go to Mary's funeral?"

Russ huffed irritably. "No, I didn't."

"Mary Travis said she saw Ida in the grocery store before Mary moved to Cold Springs," Tom continued nervously. "Said Ida looked at her funny. She just stared so hard at Mary that it set her hair on end. Wouldn't say nothing to her, but wouldn't stop staring at her."

"So, she stared at the woman!" Russ shot back, impatiently. "Big deal!"

Tom was one foolish old man if he thought he could bait Russ into admitting to any conversation he may or may not have had with either woman. Ida Green was gone. Nothing she said or did back then mattered one bit anymore and Mary Travis had been buried weeks ago. "You're fishing in an empty pond, Tom. Ida Green was a concerned and distraught mother, torn to pieces by the fact that her child shot and killed the man she loved. She was grief stricken," he reasoned. "Mary Travis was the forewoman at the trial who read the verdict. Of course Ida hated her. She hated anybody who had anything to do with her daughter's conviction, which is understandable," he quickly added. "She had a right to be angry, just like the system had a right to convict a killer for murder."

"I'm too old for this. I don't want my name associated with anything related to Desdimona or Ida Green, 'specially not in a book!"

"Why'd you call me, Tom?"

"I called to see if you knew anything about what she was going to put into that book."

"What makes you think I'd know anything about Desi Green or her book?"

Tom hesitated. "You know everything, Russ."

He hung up without saying another word to dumb-ass Tom Billings.

"What was that about?" his wife, Delilah, asked. Concern was written all over her face.

"Desi Green and her goddamned book," he said, gruffly tossing the newspaper he'd been reading on the floor of the porch.

Delilah reached over and rubbed her hand on top of his. She shook her head slowly, and then stared thoughtfully out into the yard. "Poor Olivia Gatewood," she said, solemnly. "I feel so bad for that woman." She frowned at her husband. "Remember how she looked in that courtroom? Beautiful woman, torn down, and worn out by the burden of the death of her husband, finding out about his mistress and having to sit there in the same room with that woman." She pursed her lips together. "I tell you, I couldn't have done it."

He shrugged. "Well, the man was no saint, but he didn't deserve what happened to him either."

"She's just adding insult to injury." She looked over at her husband. "Desi Green? She got so much more than she deserved." She shook her head. "She kills a man and then ends up with money from him, and now, she wants to write a book about it? Is that what's got Tom so up in arms?"

"He's worried about his reputation," Russ explained as generically as he could. "Worried about what she might write about him."

She chuckled. "He should be happy anybody's writing anything about him. Tom could end up being famous when it comes out. Add some excitement to his dull life."

Russ smiled thinly.

"She didn't shoot him!" Ida Green's anguished voice echoed through his memories. *"Desi wouldn't do this, Judge Fleming! She loved Julian and she wouldn't do this!"*

Some things spoke more clearly and loudly than a mother's pleading voice. Some outcomes were determined by bigger and greater things. Justice came in all shapes and sizes, and it didn't necessarily look the same to different people, but it was still justice nonetheless. In the end, Ida Green wasn't any different than anybody else sitting in that courtroom. She wanted justice. Russ gave her her fair share.

"Nobody wins here, Ida," he'd said to her, sitting trembling in that chair across from his desk in his chambers. *"A man's dead. An innocent man. Nobody wins. But you do as you're told, then maybe—everybody can lose a little less."*

"You think she'll write about you in her book, honey?" Delilah asked, grinning.

He tried to shrug it off as best he could. "I'm sure she's got a lot more to say in her book than to talk about an old, retired, gray-haired judge."

Lonnie

"*Dammit Jordan!*" Lonnie gasped, fisting the bedsheets. "Dammit!"

Moments later, she came all over his face.

He'd begged her to let him come over to her place. "I just want a taste, Lonnie. Won't take long."

Less than five minutes after she'd let him in, Lonnie was having the orgasm of a lifetime and he never even bothered to loosen his tie. When he was finished, Jordan stood next to the side of her bed, adjusted his necktie, and loomed over Lonnie, trembling on the bed. Jordan wiped his mouth with the back of his hand, and smiled.

"You need to wash your face," she finally recovered enough to say.

He drove his hands deep into his pockets, adding emphasis to a riveting and impressive hard-on, straining the front of his pants. "I'll see you later."

Without saying another word, Jordan turned and left, closing her front door quietly behind him.

Abigail Parker was in her forties, divorced once, married now, with five kids, two of them step. She'd been a nurse for going on fifteen years now and loved it. She loved her job, and Mrs. Gatewood. She made decent money, enough to help pay the bills, but two of her children wanted to go to college. She'd always encouraged her children to reach for the stars, and hoped that they could at least get a hand on the moon. A college education wasn't the norm in her family. Abby had gone back to school after her divorce from her first husband and she did it while taking care of two small children on her own. She couldn't even get child support from their father. But she promised herself that she'd finish and she did. It was hard but she did it. She'd worked in a hospital for a while after she'd graduated, but Abby preferred more of a caregiver role to a select few than to be on rotation in a hospital. She was good at taking care of folks. It was her passion.

"Thanks for meeting me here." The stylish woman across from her didn't even ask Abby's name when she sat down. Tall, and slender, she had curves, but not the full kind Abby had. And she wore her hair cut short like a man's, but nobody would ever mistake a woman like her for a man. Everything she had on probably cost more than Abby's car sitting out there in the parking lot.

The waiter came right over to the table and asked what she wanted to drink.

"A nice, chilled Riesling would be nice," she said, smiling.

She could've been a high fashion model, she was so beautiful, with dark and smooth skin, sparkling white teeth, and large exotic eyes.

She looked at Abby and smiled. "I hope you haven't been waiting too long," she said, apologetically.

Abby managed to smile back. "No. Not long at all."

"Well, I do appreciate your time. I know you must be busy."

A woman like her apologizing for taking up Abby's time? It seemed odd to Abby.

"I'm starving," she said, scanning the menu.

The menu had no prices on anything, which told Abby that she probably couldn't afford anything on it.

"Have you eaten here before?" *the woman asked, looking up at Abby.*

Abby would've thought that a woman like that could look at a woman like her, size her up the same way Abby had been sizing her up, and know the answer to that question without even asking.

"Afraid I haven't," *Abby smiled, sheepishly.*

The longer she sat here, the longer she realized that she had made a mistake in coming. Abby had no business talking to this woman. And a situation like this could only lead to the kind of trouble Abby didn't need. The Gatewoods were good to her. Mrs. Gatewood was the sweetest woman she'd ever worked for and the last thing she needed to do was to jeopardize the best job she'd ever had. Abby was just about to tell her that.

"The filet mignon is delicious," *the woman said, looking up at her.* "But if you prefer seafood, I'd recommend the sea bass."

"I shouldn't have come," *Abby blurted out, sorry for having wasted this woman's time.* "I really just . . ."

"I thought I explained everything thoroughly over the phone, Mrs. Parker," *the woman said, coolly.*

Abby nodded. "And this is my fault. I was too hasty in agreeing to this. I shouldn't don't need to get involved."

"You said that Mrs. Gatewood kept a box hidden under her bed?"

Abby had said that. She'd said a lot of things, all of it too much.

"She keeps it locked?"

"Her most private things are in that box. No one has any right to invade her privacy," *Abby said, adamantly.*

As polished and sophisticated as this woman was, Abby decided right then and there that she wasn't going to be a pushover with this woman. She'd expected that. She'd come here thinking that she had Abby right where she wanted her and could make her do things that she had changed her mind about doing.

The woman studied Abby long and hard, before finally reaching inside her purse, pulling out an envelope and sliding it across the table.

Abby didn't have to look inside it to know what was in it. But she wasn't going to touch it. If she did, she'd be tempted, and she'd made her mind up already.

"You could cover an awful lot of bad checks with that," the woman said.

How she'd found out about Abby floating checks was something Abby had been trying not to think about. Her husband had been out of work for months, and Abby had been robbing Peter to pay Paul, trying to keep the lights on, and food on the table. She had thousands out there in pay day loans, and two of her children desperately wanted to go to college. But that was her mess to deal with, and Mrs. Gatewood shouldn't have to pay for Abby's mess.

She met the woman's gaze and held it. "What you're asking me to do, ain't right."

The woman leaned back in her seat. "All I'm asking you to do is to look inside and come back and tell me what you saw."

"I don't want to hurt that woman," Abby said, desperately.

"If you don't tell her, and I don't tell her, then how is she going to know?"

Olivia would know. The way she took inventory of the contents of that box nearly every day . . . of course she'd know if somebody else touched it.

"Why?" Abby asked. "Why do you want me to do this?"

The woman's expression never changed. "I need to know what's in that box. It's a simple enough request, and I'm offering a lot of money for that information. Money that you need to help take care of your family. But I'm not going to force you to do anything you don't want to do."

The woman reached across the table and started to pick up her envelope. Abby had written more checks than her money could cover. Her car was a missed payment away from being repossessed. She'd gotten a notice the other day warning her that if the water bill wasn't paid by Friday they'd turn it off.

"Promise me you won't use anything in that box to hurt Mrs. Gatewood."

The woman paused, and then smiled. "I have no intention of bringing harm to Olivia Gatewood in any way, Abby."

Abby had kept her end of the bargain. She'd described every item in Olivia's secret box, and she took her time getting to the best part, the only thing in that box that mattered was the last thing she'd mentioned.

"In the bottom, underneath everything else," she explained slowly over the phone, "were two birth certificates."

"One for each of her children," Lonnie naturally concluded.

"Both for Jordan," Abby finally admitted after a long pause.

"Two birth certificates? One's a copy?"

"One's different."

Lonnie waited for the woman to elaborate, but obviously she wasn't going to. Not without some coaching. "Come on, Abby. You've crossed the line already." It was almost a threat. "You can't turn back now. What's the difference between the two documents?"

Abby sighed deeply before finally responding. "The birth-father's name."

Lonnie often wondered if he knew? Even if he did, Jordan would take a secret like that to the grave with him before he'd let it get out. And if he didn't, maybe . . . he should.

Go Up to the Devil

"*Mr. Jones.*"

Solomon looked up at Jordan Gatewood standing over him and his dinner date. Reluctantly, he stood up, and shook the man's hand.

"Mr. Gatewood."

Was it a coincidence that he and Jordan Gatewood happened to be at the same restaurant, or was he just plain lucky?

The man stood a good three to four inches taller than Solomon. He was a big dude, looking every bit the football player he'd been twenty-five years ago in college. They'd never met face-to-face, but Jordan knew his name. Solomon found it profound, to say the least.

Jordan glanced at the woman sitting at the table.

"Mya, this is Jordan Gatewood," Solomon said, introducing the two of them. "Mya Richards," he said to Jordan.

"Nice to meet you," Mya said.

Jordan ignored her and turned his attention back to Solomon.

"You negotiated the terms and conditions of Desi Green's contract with the publisher." It wasn't a question.

He waited for Solomon to respond.

"I'm sure it was just business."

"Of course it was just business," Solomon finally said.

"My family and I have been through our fair share of heartache and scrutiny, Mr. Jones, which I'm sure you're aware of."

"I am," he said, tersely.

"My concern has always been for the women in my family, my mother and my sister. I've worked hard to try and protect them from the fallout from my father's death. It hasn't always been easy, but I've done the best I could," he explained coolly.

Solomon wasn't fooled by the calm demeanor of Gatewood. Never trust an opponent, whether fighting in the ring or in the courtroom or even here, standing over a dinner table. That was his mantra. "Believe me. I understand, and I empathize."

A dangerous darkness filled Jordan's eyes. "Then empathize with this. Desi Green is not to mention my name, or my family's name in that goddamned book of hers," he threatened.

"I have no idea what she's going to put in her book, and it's none of my business," Solomon said, defensively.

"Now, it is your business." He glared at him. "That bitch is like a fuckin' rat in my attic that I can't get rid of," he said threateningly. "She took apart my family, and then got out of prison and took our dignity."

He was referring to the money.

"Dumb move on her part. She should've counted her blessings, all twenty million of them and faded away. The fact that anybody would pay her money to talk about how she shot and killed a man is the real crime. But I can't stop them from making the offer."

"No. You can't."

The longer Jordan talked, the more angry Solomon found himself becoming. The arrogant bastard sounded like he owned the whole damn world and everyone in it. The air surrounding Gatewood became stagnant and cold. And all of a sudden Solomon realized that Gatewood didn't do coincidences. He'd found out that Solomon was here and decided to show up.

Jordan glared at him. "Desi's on the wrong playing field and she's out of her league. So far, she's been lucky and the ball's bounced in her favor, but it's just luck and it won't last forever."

Solomon rolled his eyes at Gatewood's tired metaphor. "Desi served her time, Mr. Gatewood. The system set her free. *Free* is the operative word here."

"As long as she and I breathe the same air, neither one of us will ever be free. If you care about Desi, and it seems that you do, then you'll give her my message. If the name Gatewood comes up in that book, she will regret it. And prison will be like a country club compared to what could happen if she's not careful."

Solomon glared at the man. "There's no law against telling her side of her own story."

"There is when it bumps into mine. You give her my message." Jordan pushed past Solomon and left the restaurant.

Another Round

Tom Billings drank too much. His wife, Lola, had forbidden him to drink in the house, so he drank at Ed's, a small bar uptown. They knew him at Ed's. Ed Kowalski, the owner, had been a close and personal friend of his before he died a few years back. His daughter, Sabrina, ran the place now.

"You know the rules, Bree," he said, turning up the last of his glass to finish what was left of his beer. He burped and sat the glass on the bar counter. "I shouldn't have to ask."

Sabrina, or Bree, came over without saying a word, smiled, and filled his glass again.

Tom had retired seven years ago and he still couldn't find anything to do with himself. The mayor hadn't given him a choice in the matter.

"You're sixty-five, Tom. Time for you to go," he'd told him. "We can have a ceremony if you'd like. You can invite your family and friends. It would be real nice."

"If you don't mind, Art," Tom sighed, dismally. "Why don't you just give me that cheap-ass gold watch here, and I can go on home."

He'd tried doing other things since he'd retired. Tom had started up a small handyman business. He'd even had business cards printed up and a logo painted on the side of his truck. That lasted for all of about six months, before he got the hint that he didn't work fast enough or cheap enough for people around here. Next, he decided to work on restoring that old Caprice he'd had sitting in the garage for twenty years that he'd been promising he'd work on once he had the time. He worked on that for about three months before he got bored with it, and left it sitting up on blocks in pieces with Lola threatening to have it hauled off to the junkyard.

He was seventy-two now. His body wasn't what it used to be, but he was proud to say that his mind was as sharp as ever, and he was seriously considering putting it to good use, doing what he knew how to do best, and start some kind of private investigation business.

"Hello," Bree said to the man sliding onto the bar stool next to Tom. "What can I get you?"

"Scotch on the rocks, please."

Tom had never seen him before. He looked rather young. Tom guessed him to be in his thirties. He had on an expensive-looking button-down, and a pair of fancy jeans. He knew they were fancy because they weren't Levi's or Wrangler. As far as Tom was concerned, everything else was considered "designer."

"You new to Blink?" Tom asked, feeling the effects of the six beers he'd had already.

The man nodded. "Yes. As a matter of fact, I am."

Tom extended his hand. "Tom Billings," he introduced himself.

"Dan Freeman," he replied.

He carefully studied the man's features without trying. Tom was observant to a fault. "You just passing through or got family here?" he probed, casually.

Old habits died hard. He'd be the first person to admit to that. Seven years after retiring, operating in cop mode was still second nature. Tom was a sponge, soaking up everything about everyone. It's what made him so good at remembering names and putting them with faces.

"I'm here on business, actually."

Tom looked surprised. "Business?" He chuckled. "What kind of business would bring you to a place like Blink, Texas?"

Bree sat the man's drink down in front of him. He took a sip before answering. "I'm a reporter," he finally admitted.

Tom sighed irritably. He hated reporters. Hell, everybody in Blink hated reporters. During the Gatewood murder trial, the city was filled with their rude and obnoxious asses, shoving microphones in people's faces and then making up answers when they didn't get the ones they wanted.

Tom grunted, and gulped down his drink.

The man shrugged. "From that response, I take it that you don't like reporters?"

"I really don't," he said, nonchalantly.

"Sorry to hear that."

"Where you from?"

"Corpus."

"Well, I hate to tell you this, but you've wasted a trip." Of course, Tom knew why the man was here. Desi Green's name drew reporters to Blink, like shit drew flies. "She doesn't live here anymore."

The man turned to Tom. "Who?"

"You know who I'm talking about. That woman can't wipe her ass without some reporter wanting to write about it. Desi Green moved out of Blink when she got her inheritance. So, like I said, you've wasted your gas coming up here."

"I don't know anything about any Desi Green, Tom. I'm here chasing a lead on a story bubbling up in South Texas."

Tom stared at him to see if he was lying. "What lead? What story?"

"A lead on a trafficking story involving illegally transporting non-U.S. citizens from Mexico into this country and then selling them off to the highest bidder as slaves." He stared hard at Tom. "I've been working on it for months, and my investigation has led me here."

The sound of the world crashing down all around him was deafeningly quiet. Tom's throat suddenly went dry. His palms broke out in a sweat, and his heart beat hard enough to shake him in his seat. But anything he felt inside was invisible on the outside. Tom didn't flinch.

"It seems that there is a very large and intricate human trafficking network responsible for sneaking people into this country with the promise of new jobs and education. But once these people cross the border, they become property. They're set up in safe houses, hidden from society. Families are separated. The men are shipped off to orchard farms as pickers, some of the women are sold off as domestics, while other women and children are sold into sex rings."

Tom swallowed. "And your investigation led you here?" He didn't like the way this Dan Freeman was looking at him.

"Go figure," Dan said, unemotionally. "Of all places."

"Why here?" he eventually managed to ask. Blink, Texas, was too specific a place. Most people had never heard of it and couldn't tell you where to find it on a map. So, how would this reporter find it? And how'd he find Tom?

"Before she was picked up for prostitution and deported, a young lady named Alicia told a tearful and fascinating story to authorities about how her parents sent her here, illegally, on the promise that her sponsors in this country would enroll her in an American university where she could learn to become a doctor. They paid a thousand dollars of their hard-earned money to get her across the border."

Tom didn't remember an Alicia.

"She never made it to college. Instead, she was beaten, raped, and put out on the streets to work."

Tom swallowed. "Poor kid," he muttered.

"Yeah, well, as it turned out, Alicia was a smart kid with a photographic memory, and she memorized the license plate number of the truck that she and other girls were ordered into once they crossed the border."

Tom took another long gulp of his beer.

"She must've been pretty convincing because authorities traced that plate number to a rental agency just outside of town here. Whoever rented that truck, though, was pretty smart. He used the I.D. of a man who'd been dead for years. The man had died of a heart attack in jail."

Tom scavenged up enough courage to look the man in the face. His heart pounded so hard, it surprised him that no one else in the room could feel it. Lies came quickly to him when he was a younger man. Now, he had to look a little harder inside himself to find them.

"I know just about everybody in town," he said. "And I can't imagine anybody here would have anything to do with kidnapping."

The cold blue of that reporter's eyes sliced right through Tom. "If I've learned anything in my line of work, I've learned that people are capable of just about anything. Nothing surprises me anymore where human nature is concerned. Absolutely nothing."

Tom turned his attention back to his beer, finished it off, and waved to Bree to close out his tab. He put money down on the counter, and then stood up to leave. "I, uh . . . wish you luck with your investigation," he said as he was leaving.

"No need," Freeman said. "I'm pretty damn good at what I do. Luck is inconsequential."

Tom wanted to blame his weak knees on the beer, but he'd be lying to himself. He'd spent too many years trying to be all things, to cover all his bases, justifying every decision he'd ever made and calling it righteous. Ultimately, God decided what was right and what was wrong. Tom had made it work for him as long as he could, obliviously God had finally stepped in to take over.

In My Father's House

"Your son's catch of that seventy-eight-yard winning touchdown pass was nothing short of amazing, Mr. Gatewood. How's it make you feel to know that he won the game for the team, your alma mater?"

Jordan had received another e-mail from an anonymous source again. He watched the clip of an interview of his father that happened shortly after his team had won the Cotton Bowl. Played in real time, the interview of Julian looked normal enough. But whoever sent the video had slowed the film down to a frame-by-frame shot between the time that the reporter shoved that microphone under Julian's nose and when he started his answer. In those few moments, Jordan saw, the apprehension and disappointment in Julian's eyes that spoke volumes.

"I feel proud," Julian said, *enthusiastically. "But then, I'm proud of all of my children."*

The rift between Jordan and his father had been thick Jordan's whole life. When he was a kid, he had no way to articulate the distance he felt from his father, but as he grew older, and saw the bond between Julian and Jordan's sister, he knew that he would never be able to live up to his father's expectations, not even if he walked on water.

At the end of the clip, a song began to play from that same file.

> *Papa was a rolling stone!*
> *Wherever he laid his hat was his home!*

His family was brilliant at keeping secrets. Obviously, somebody had left the door open with this one. Besides Jordan, his mother, and Julian, another person knew this secret and thought to torment him with it. Maybe they were planning on trying to extort money from him, in exchange for his silence. He was head of the Gatewood family, and its fortune. What would he stand to lose if the media got ahold of this?

Jordan paused and stared at the frozen frame of Julian's face before finally pressing the delete key. Julian was a motherfucker. Olivia had loved him despite of it. He wondered what Julian had been to Ida. Did she love him blindly, too, or was she infatuated by the money? He'd left that woman millions, but you'd never know it from the way she lived. Ida Green didn't run out and buy a new car or a big house. For all he knew, she never spent a dime of that money. So, if it wasn't for his money . . . Women were too damn silly sometimes.

The truth was, Jordan hadn't inherited his father's millions, Olivia had. But when she became ill, she signed over power of attorney to him and he'd been in charge of the part of the estate that hadn't been willed to charities, or Ida Green. So, technically, it wasn't his inheritance that was the issue. It was his position, his reputation, and his honor. And those things were priceless as long as he kept his last name.

In the Deep

In person, Desi Green was beautiful. There was no missing the un-canny resemblance to her mother, Ida, but Desi was breathtaking. At forty-four, the woman had the skin of a toddler. Sue's natural investigative prowess identified every designer brand that the woman had on within thirty seconds of meeting her: dark wash 7 For All Mankind skinny jeans; Manolo Blahnik quilted ballerina flats; a basic, white T-shirt that probably cost more than most people paid for an entire wardrobe; and making Sue drool, dangling from Desi's delicate wrist was a David Yurman Blue Oval Mosaic Cuff bracelet.

Sue had agreed to meet Desi at her hotel suite at the Trump Tower, overlooking New York's Central Park. She'd expected to meet Desi the ex-con, a brow-beaten and sullen woman, awkward with how to live in her newfound wealth, but Desi had an unexpected air of sophistication about her that caught Sue off guard, and the woman looked as if she'd had that money all her life.

"Thank you for agreeing to come to New York," Sue said after the two of them settled down in the main living area of Desi's suite. "It's good to meet face-to-face with my collaborators." She smiled. "It helps me to get to know you better, and I hope we can do this a couple of times during the course of writing this book together."

Desi smiled confidently. "I've never been to New York. I'm glad I came."

"Are you nervous?"

Desi took a deep breath. "I'm ready to do this. I need to do this."

"That's what I want to hear. I know it's not easy, but I've done this plenty of times, and whatever I can do to help you get through it, well . . . that's what I'm here for."

"How much do you want to know? What are my limitations?"

Sue shook her head. "You have none. It's up to you. How far are you willing to go?"

Without hesitation, Desi gave her answer. "I'm ready to tell everything, Sue. As hard as this is going to be, it's been harder keeping it all to myself, all these years."

"Why have you kept it all to yourself for so long?"

"In the beginning," Desi's expression turned introspective, "I was scared to open my mouth. I had everybody in my ear telling me not to say anything, from Momma to that lawyer, even Sheriff Billings told me that I had a right to be silent and if I was smart, it would be in my best interest to make good use of it."

"And what about later, when you were in prison and then after you were finally released?"

She shrugged. "Nothing mattered when I was locked up. I was just trying to get through each day, and trying not to spend too much time dwelling on what got me there. When I got out, things just happened so fast. Suddenly, I was trying to find somebody in Blink, Texas to hire me, wishing I was back in prison because at least I had electricity and running water. I had three meals a day. For the first time in my life, there was nobody to take care of me, not Momma and not prison. I was on my own, and it was up to me to take care of me."

"And when the money came?"

She sighed. "I don't know. It was a lot like winning the lottery, I guess. One day you've got nothing and the next, you've got more than you know what to do with. Most people can't tell you how they'd feel or act if all of a sudden they had millions of dollars after being as broke as I was."

"How'd you feel?"

"At first, I thought, good—great! I can get the lights turned on now, and maybe even buy me a car. But as soon as I realized that I was happy, I got scared. I thought somebody was playing a bad joke on me, and the next day, the Gatewoods had their lawyers put a stop on the inheritance. All of a sudden, not only was I broke again, but I was backed up against the wall by people I thought I'd never see or hear from again. I felt trapped, and like they owned me, and they could do whatever they wanted to do to me."

"Obviously, you don't feel that way anymore," Sue said, hesitantly.

"It's not from their lack of trying," Desi admitted.

"I take it they're not happy about this book?"

"No."

"Are they worried about what you'll tell me?"

Desi nodded. "They are worried, and they should be."

Sue's heart skipped an excited beat. She'd only ever hoped that Desi would give her a firsthand account of what happened the night she shot and killed Julian Gatewood, what her life was like before, and after.

Now, Desi was implying that Sue could possibly get more than she bargained for.

"So, what happened to change your mind and tell your story? When did you accept the fact that they didn't own you, as you put it?"

"When Jordan Gatewood looked me in the eyes, and I saw that he was afraid."

Sue was speechless.

"He's good at hiding it, at puffing up his chest and strutting around like he's cock of the walk. He didn't mean for me to see it, and I didn't let on that I did. I know what his weakness is, and he's afraid that I'll expose it."

Sue's eyes widened. "He's a powerful man, and powerful men can be dangerous."

Experience had taught her how to fish for and pull out the conflict in people, between people. Sue was using that experience to her advantage here to expose the tension between Desi and Jordan.

Desi leaned forward, balanced her elbows on her thighs, and stared at Sue straight in the eyes. "He is because everybody thinks he is," she explained earnestly. "I believed he was, but now I know better. Jordan's like a scared dog backed into a corner, snarling, and growling. If you reach for him, he'll bite you."

"So you think he's afraid of you?" There was no way in hell that a man like Jordan Gatewood could ever be afraid of pretty, petite Desi Green, no matter how rich she was.

Desi surprised Sue and smiled. "I finally do."

As much as she didn't want to be, Sue was suddenly afraid for Desi. She didn't know what Desi had over Gatewood, but whatever it was, Sue knew that she was about to embark on a journey that she hadn't expected at all.

"What do you mean by that?" Sue asked, intently.

"Other women who were locked up used to tell me to be glad that I didn't get the death penalty, especially for killing that rich man." Desi leaned back. A strange calm washed over her. "They should've given me the death penalty and gone through with it because as long as I was locked up, so was the truth. Now that I'm out, it has to come out too."

Sugar Wishes

Desi finished pulling on her thigh-high leather boots, stood up, and looked herself over in the mirror.

"I was born to wear these," she said, admiringly.

Lonnie came over and stood next to her. "Amen to that."

"You think I'm too old for these?"

"Old is a state of mind, Desi."

"Twenty-year-olds wear boots like these."

Lonnie shook her head. "No. Twenty-year-olds can't afford them."

The sales associate appeared like magic, out of nowhere.

"I'll take two pair," Desi said, loving the way she looked. "A black pair and a brown pair."

"Do you have red?" Lonnie chimed in.

The sales woman smiled. "No red."

"Size eight," Desi said.

"I'll wrap them up as soon as you get them off," the woman said.

Desi shook her head. "No. I want to wear them."

Lonnie nodded her approval. "Good move, girl."

After shopping, Lonnie gave the driver directions to a Cuban restaurant called Favela Cubana located in the West Village. Lonnie had braised skirt steak, bell peppers, Spanish onions, white rice, and black beans. Desi decided on half the rotisserie chicken, with Brazilian passion fruit, white rice, black beans, and Favela sauce.

"I'd like to make a toast." Lonnie raised her bottle of Red Stripe and waited for Desi to do the same. "Here's to whatever it is that's got you lit up like a Christmas tree."

"New York City, baby." Desi laughed. "What took me so long to get out of Texas?"

"Hell if I know. You should've left as soon as you got your inheritance. But no. You stuck to Texas like a fly to flypaper."

"I'm not staying stuck, though."

"I know an excellent Realtor. We could find you a nice little one-bedroom in the Village for next to nothing."

Desi frowned. "What's next to nothing in New York City?"

Lonnie shrugged. "Couple million."

"For a one-bedroom apartment?" Desi shrieked.

Lonnie raised her beer again. "Here's to the big apple."

"The big apple!"

"And to Sue Parker's nosey ass."

Desi laughed. "Sue."

"To them bad-ass thigh-high boots!"

"They're made for walking, girl."

Lonnie's expression turned somber. "To Ida Green and Mr. J."

Desi was definitely caught off guard with that one. But in a surprisingly good way. "May they rest in peace."

"And to Mary Travis." Lonnie stared intently.

Desi paused. "May God have mercy on her soul."

She meant that.

"You gonna tell me why you came all the way to New York?" Desi finally asked.

"To watch you buy those boots." Lonnie stuffed a piece of steak into her mouth.

"I'm serious, Lonnie. You didn't fly all the way up here just to see me shop."

"How's the book coming along?"

"It's coming. Stop trying to change the subject."

"I'm not changing the subject. I'm leading into it."

"What's that mean?"

"It means that I have some information that might make this book of yours even more riveting, darling!"

Desi put down her fork. "Information on the judge?"

Lonnie rolled her eyes. "Like he's the only fish in the sea worth frying." She cut into her steak again. "You know, you really need to think in broader strokes than that, Des."

"Okay, so what information and on who?"

She finally put down her knife and fork and leaned closer to Desi. "Okay, so we're a team in this, right?"

Desi laughed. "What, like in a basketball game or something?"

Lonnie didn't find it funny. "I'm really putting my ass on the line for you, Desi."

"You keep saying that," Desi responded, not too keen on Lonnie's tone.

"Because it's true. I'm calling in a ton of favors for you, girl. Sticking my neck out in ways you can't even imagine."

"I never asked you to do any of this, Lonnie."

She surprised Desi and smiled. "I do it because I care. Because you're closer to me than any sister could be. I do it because I feel I have to."

Lonnie sent weird signals sometimes. She was cool, but then there were moments, like this one, when she wasn't quite sure where Lonnie was coming from. She said, one thing with her mouth, but the expression in her eyes sent a whole other kind of message.

"So, what'd you want to tell me?"

"Tom Billings," she blurted out.

Desi raised her eyebrows. "Sheriff Tom Billings?"

Lonnie smiled triumphantly. "One in the same."

"What about him?"

"If I tell you, will you promise to put it in the book?"

"What is it, Lonnie?" Desi asked, suspiciously.

"I want you to put this in the book," Lonnie challenged.

"Tell me what it is, first."

Lonnie looked pissed. "Turns out he's as dirty as the judge."

Desi's chin dropped. "He's a pedophile?"

"Turns out the good sheriff is, or at least, was part of a human-trafficking ring, sneaking illegals across the border and then selling them like property."

Desi couldn't believe it. It was one thing for the judge to be crooked, but the sheriff, too? That was just too much of a coincidence, and it didn't feel right. "How do you know?"

Lonnie obviously didn't like being challenged. "How do I always know?"

"Another contact?"

"Cops traced a license plate number of the truck hauling illegals into the country to a rental car company outside your beloved Blink. The car had been rented by some dead guy, a homeless guy who died in jail. His I.D. and other belongings were supposed to have been secured in the police custody locker."

"It wasn't?"

"Billings took it."

"But, how do you know he took it, Lonnie. You have proof?"

"Fuck, Desi!" Lonnie blurted out. "Don't be dumb! Hell, yeah, I have proof. I wouldn't be telling you this if I didn't have proof!"

For a minute, Desi thought Lonnie might swing at her. Desi braced herself.

"You need to keep your damn voice down, Lonnie!" Desi warned.

"And you need to remember who the hell I am!" Lonnie glared at her. "I don't make this shit up, especially when I'm putting my ass. . . ."

"On the line," Desi snapped. "Yeah, I know."

Before Lonnie could respond, the waiter appeared at the table. "You two ladies doing okay? You need a refill on those drinks?"

"Can you just bring us the check, please?" Desi asked.

"Sure thing."

Lonnie used the time to compose herself. "I promise you, Desi. I'm not making this up. I don't operate that way. You should know that."

Desi had calmed down too. "I do know that. But if I'm going to include this in the book, I need something solid to go on. Sue's going to ask for proof."

Lonnie grinned. "So you do believe me?"

Desi nodded. "I do. It's just . . . I can't believe the kind of people we're dealing with. They call me a criminal, point the finger at me, and make me feel like dirt. Those bastards have put me under a microscope for the whole world to see. Now, I'm going to let them see how it feels."

The waiter brought the bill and Lonnie grabbed it before Desi had a chance to. "Lunch is on me. You just talk to the writer. I'll get you your proof."

"You can't prove this," Sue said after hearing Desi's insight into the life and times of Tom Billings. "I thought I made it clear from the beginning, Desi, that this book is about you, about your experiences. I'm not writing a tabloid. If you have information like this, then you need to take it to the police. Get even that way, but don't use me to do it."

Desi couldn't believe what she was hearing. Sue wanted a story. Desi was giving her a story. Now, she was telling Desi that she didn't want this story? Desi was giving her just a hint of the scandal that had plagued her life. Billings wasn't the good, upstanding representative of the law that he'd led everyone to believe he was. And yet, he'd put handcuffs on Desi.

"You want the victim," Desi said, finally understanding where Sue's disapproval was coming from. "You want the soap opera that's been Desi Green for the last twenty-six years. I thought you wanted the truth, Sue."

"Do you want people to take this book seriously? We put this in it, Desi, and it becomes trash. Slander and scandal. Is that what you want?"

Desi swallowed, and stared, insulted, at Sue. "I want to expose them the way they exposed me. I want to peel back the layers of their lives, and put them on display the way they did me."

"So, you hire some detective to dig up dirt on Tom Billings and give him as good as he gave you?"

Desi stared long and hard at Sue before finally responding. "Bottom line, it's my book, Sue."

"My name's on the cover too, Desi. My reputation is at stake, maybe even more than yours."

"And I'm not signing off on any book that I don't approve of." Desi stood up, walked over to the door, and held it open for Sue to leave. "Anytime you want your advance money back, you let me know."

Sue stopped before leaving. "Even if it is true, exposing him like this makes you no better than he is. Don't you see that?"

"All I see is a chance to clean up after my name, and showing everybody the dirt that's on his."

Sue left without saying good-bye, but without asking for her money back.

Their Crooked Mile

"*I got something* in the mail."

Tom Billings sounded like he was drunk. His voice cracked and he was slurring.

"Tom," Russ said, rubbing sleep from his eyes. "It's after two in the morning. Why don't you go sleep it off and call me tomorrow at a more reasonable hour."

"It's a picture of me and some . . . some kids, Russ." His voice trailed off.

Russ sat up on the side of the bed.

"Russ?" his wife asked, sleepily. "What is it?"

"Just Tom, honey. He's a little drunk. Go back to sleep."

She moaned. "Take the phone downstairs, please," she said irritably.

Russ got up and left the room. "What kids, Tom?"

Tom sighed irritably. "You know good and damn well what kids."

Russ fought back the panic that started to grow in his chest. Something was going on. "Who sent it?"

Tom hesitated. "I don't know."

"Well is there a return address, a P.O. box, something?" Russ said, angrily.

"I said I don't know who sent it, Russ! It's just . . ."

Russ took a deep breath to calm himself and hopefully it was deep enough to calm Tom's fears too. "It's just a picture? A picture of you and some kids," he said, trying to rationalize the situation. "So what?"

"I knew it would come to this," Tom said, woefully. "I knew it."

"What the hell are you talking about?" Russ asked frustrated. He filled a small shot glass with scotch, and drank it quickly.

Tom was so quiet on the other end of the phone that Russ thought he had hung up, or passed out. "You mess around with the devil long enough, Russ, and sooner or later, he'll beat you."

Russ grimaced. "You're fuckin' drunk off your ass!" he growled. "Go to sleep, Tom."

"Ida Green cursed us, Russ." Tom chuckled menacingly. "She cursed us the day we put her daughter away in prison."

Now, the man was just talking nonsense. "Ida Green's dead and buried in the ground. She ain't in the business of cursing anybody these days."

"We got greedy, Russ," Tom continued, unaffected by anything coming out of Russ's mouth. "I knew it in my gut that someday—somehow it would come back to bite us in the ass."

Russ hadn't given energy to a single thought about Ida or about what had happened back then. Shit, too much time had passed to care. Desi Green was out, and ended up being a very rich woman.

"We saved that girl's life," Russ explained.

"We took it. And we kept on taking lives, Russ. For too long. Too many."

Rage flushed over Russ like a heat wave. "Don't you put that shit on me, Tom! Don't you even think of trying to put what you did on me!"

"You reaped the benefits of what I did, Russ," he said, quietly.

"Fuck you! What I do ain't illegal! It ain't a crime if two people are consenting adults!"

Tom chuckled. "And that's the rub, ain't it? They tell you what you want to hear, and it makes it fine as wine in your mind? Is that how it works, Russ?"

Russ rubbed sleep from his eyes. Tom was a fuckin' alcoholic, and tonight he was drunk and talking out of the side of his head about nonsense. "What's in the picture, Tom? So, it's you and some kids. What? Are you beating the kids? Eating them? Stuffing them into burlap sacks and tossing them in the river? What?"

Again, Tom was quiet, and the empty sound on the phone was deafening. "I'm just . . . taking the kids. I'm taking them—putting them in the truck." An anguished sob crossed the phone lines. "I think she sent it." Tom finally admitted out loud, a thought that had probably been driving him crazy ever since he found out that Desi Green was writing that book.

"How? Tom, how could she know?" Russ asked with desperation. In his mind, she couldn't know a thing about either of them. Desi was nothing. She was just—a woman who's suffered under some unfortunate circumstances in her life, but that was such a long time ago. Russ and Tom were probably nothing more than distant memories to that woman.

"You remember," Tom started to say, drifting off onto another conversation. "You remember how Ida cried that day? You remember how she begged and cried . . ."

Russ squeezed his eyes shut trying to block out a memory he thought was long gone.

"She begged us, Russ. . . . Begged us to . . ."

"You know she didn't do this!" Ida's eyes were bloodshot red. She was on her knees, for crying out loud. On her knees tugging at Tom, and then she crawled across the floor to Russ.

Tom had called Russ when he'd gotten the call from the Gatewood lawyers. "I don't know what to do. I don't know what—"

"Oh, God!" Ida sobbed. "Tom—Tom, please! Judge Russ! She's just a baby! She's my baby!"

It was hard to watch. Deep down, conscience convicted both men, but not enough.

"Sign your statement, Ida," Tom told her, after looking at Russ. "You have to sign it."

"No!" Ida shook her head so hard and fast that she nearly fell over. "No! I won't! I ain't signing nothing! 'Cause you know it's a lie!" She struggled to her feet, and took a defiant stance in front of both men. Ida pointed. "You know it's a lie! And you know it! And I ain't signing a motha fuckin' thing!"

Finally, Russ stepped forward. "You sign it, Ida, or I swear to God I'll put the death penalty on the table when it comes time to convict that girl!" He stood nose to nose with her. "And you know just like I know that the jury will find her guilty!"

Tom pulled out the chair for her. Ida deflated right before their eyes, and she signed the document.

It hadn't affected him back then. Russ stood in the middle of his kitchen feeling like he'd been bathed in mud. Ida had inherited some of Julian Gatewood's money, but not enough to keep her daughter out of prison.

"Take me instead," she said, solemnly, sitting down at that table over the statement she was supposed to sign. "She's too young. Take me." Her voice trailed off.

Tom shifted uneasily from one foot to the other. "I've got witnesses who saw her with the gun in her hand, Ida."

She looked up at him with hooded, red eyes. Tom turned away. Ida signed her official statement.

"Men like us take liberties with people's lives, Russ." Tom spoke unemotionally into the phone. "We're not gods, but we pretend to be. We have no right to do the things we do."

"You need to get some sleep, Tom. It's late."

Tom sighed. "It is late. Too damn late, and we're about to be held accountable for all our trespasses, Russ. Just like Mary. You get ready."

Tom was drunk. And he was being eaten alive by his guilt over something that had happened too long ago to matter anymore. He just needed to sleep it off, and he'd be fine in the morning. "Tom, call me in the—"

The sound of the gun going off startled Russ to the point that he dropped the phone on the floor. He stared at it, lying at his feet. His heart pounded in his throat. He slowly bent down to pick it up.

"Tom?" he asked, over and over again, but his friend didn't answer. Tom Billings was dead.

Handle Me

Mary Travis was close to eighty when she died. She'd lost both kidneys and was on dialysis, had suffered a debilitating stroke and several heart attacks, but it was a fall that killed her. She'd tripped on an area rug, fell, and hit her head on the corner of the solid mahogany coffee table.

"The coroner said she'd been dead nearly a day before someone finally found her," Solomon's mother said, somberly. She'd come by the house to go through the last of Mary's things.

Mary had raised Solomon's mother and her two sisters after their mother had died and their father left them, claiming he'd send for them as soon as he found a job out in Colorado, but he never did.

"It just breaks my heart knowing she laid there, unable to move or to call for help, and all alone." She shook her head. "Mary was loved by too many people to have been left alone."

Mother Mary, he and his cousins had all called her. Solomon had spent so much time over here that he had almost forgotten what his own home looked like. Mary made cakes from scratch, let him help wash clothes on that old scrubbing board she had and crank the handle to that antique washing machine with the rollers that you had to feed the clothes through manually.

Solomon's mother picked up what looked like an old photo album or scrapbook, and a photo fell onto the floor. He picked it up, and was shocked by what he saw, a faded school picture of Desi Green smiling back at him, wearing a white sweater underneath a plaid vest, and a plastic headband holding back thick curls. He flipped it over and read the cursive handwriting on the back.

To Miss Mary. Love Desi, age 16

"You know who that is?" his mother asked, looking over his shoulder.

"She looks familiar." He swallowed, not seeing the need to tell his mother who she was.

"That's Desi Green," his mother announced.

He looked at her.

"The one that killed that rich man, Gatewood," she continued. "Mary was on that jury that convicted her. She was the forewoman."

After packing up Mary's things and moving them across town to his mother's shed behind the house, Solomon called Desi as soon as he said his good-byes and climbed back in behind the wheel of his car.

"Solomon?" she answered.

"Hey, Desi," he said, reluctantly.

As soon as she answered he knew he'd made a mistake in calling her. Solomon should've thought this through better before giving into impulse and dialing her number. He was usually more levelheaded than this. When things didn't add up, he'd wait, analyze, and usually discover that nothing was as it seemed on the surface.

"Um . . . how are you doing?" she asked, trying not to hide the fact that she was surprised to hear from him.

"Good. I'm good."

"Is there something wrong?"

Solomon sat in his car parked outside of his mother's house. "No. Yes, Desi. I think there is something wrong."

He replayed the last few minutes in his head of the first time he and Desi met and he had told her that he was on his way to Mary's funeral.

"Mary Travis." He said her name slowly, carefully, so as not to leave any room for misinterpretation. "I thought you said you didn't know Mary Travis, Desi."

She paused. "I don't."

He clenched his teeth and forced his composure to remain in check. Solomon hated being lied to, and Desi was lying. "That day in my office, when I told you that I had a funeral to attend, and you asked whose funeral. Do you remember that?"

Again with the hesitation. "Vaguely, Solomon."

"I remember you asking me whose funeral I was attending."

"Then maybe I did. I—I don't know."

"She had your picture, Desi. A picture of you when you were sixteen," he explained like he was presenting an argument in court. "You wrote on the back, 'To Miss Mary. Love Desi.'"

Desi was silent, which confirmed everything that he needed to know.

"You lied about knowing her. Why?"

The less she said, the more her silence sparked his anger, and his curiosity. "Desi? Answer me."

"I have to go," she suddenly said.

"Where are you?"

"I'm in Manhattan," she snapped.

"We need to talk, Desi. Face-to-face."

"I said I'm in New York, Solomon."

"Where?"

Again with the silent treatment and then, not surprisingly, she hung up.

The next call he made was to his assistant. Solomon apologized profusely for interrupting her Sunday afternoon before telling her the reason for his call.

"I don't care if you have to call every hotel in Manhattan, find out which one she's checked in to and call me back."

"Today?"

"To-fuckin-day!"

The next afternoon, Solomon sat on that plane heading to JFK, wondering if he wasn't just overreacting. Maybe it wasn't as big a deal as he was making it, and Desi had simply forgotten that she had known Mary. A lot had happened to that woman since she was sixteen. It could've been that Desi didn't want to complicate things between her and Solomon considering that at the time he first mentioned his aunt Mary to her, the two of them had just met and he had made it clear that he was reluctant to work with her. Over time, he could've found all those reasons compelling enough to justify why she wouldn't tell him that she knew Mary. But what he couldn't let go of, and the thing that had convinced him that he needed to buy a ticket and get on a flight to New York and talk to her face-to-face, was the fact that Mary Travis had stood before the court, and a room full of people, and announced that the jury had found Desi guilty. What he couldn't make sense of was the fact that Mary was a member of that jury in the first place if she and the defendent knew each other.

A day after finding that picture and talking to Desi over the phone, he found himself standing at the door to her hotel room.

Of course she was shocked to see him. "Solomon. What are you—"

He didn't wait to be invited inside.

He tossed his overnight bag on the couch, crossed his arms, stood in the middle of the room and stared at Desi. "Help me to make sense of this in my head, Desi."

To Desi it wasn't really that hard. He knew that Desi and Mary did know each other and that Desi had lied to him about it. To her, it seemed pretty cut and dry.

"I don't know what you want me to say, Solomon," she shrugged. "So, I knew her. I don't see what the big deal is."

Never let them see you sweat. Before she was locked up, as scared as she was, Desi had damn near sweated herself to death. But she'd learned some things in the system. She'd learned to keep her cool even when trouble was staring her down. She'd learned to look people in the eye and to never back down if she could help it. Hell! Desi had learned to be a real superhero in that place.

He buried his hands in his pockets. The intensity in his dark eyes made her knees weak, and not in a good way.

"Tell me how you knew Mary."

She felt like her stomach was being gripped and held between two fists. "She substituted at my school one semester when one of my teachers was on maternity leave," she admitted.

He studied Desi, searching for signs that she wasn't telling the truth. Maybe even trying to find hidden truths between the lines of what she'd said. But Mary had been a substitute teacher at Desi's school. Desi liked Mary, and she thought that Mary liked her too.

"Why didn't you just tell me that?" he asked, accusingly.

Desi shrugged. "It was easier not to, I guess." She crossed the room and sat down. "We'd just met, and you'd already had your mind made up about me, Solomon. I just figured—it was easier not to talk about it."

She wished he'd sit down. At least if he did, she wouldn't feel like she was on trial again.

"Do you want some water?" she asked, all of a sudden.

"No."

"I've got cookies," she said, quickly. "Want some cookies?"

"She announced the guilty verdict at your trial, Desi," he said, coolly. "You trying to tell me that that was no big deal too?"

Desi's eyes widened. "How did you—"

"Doesn't matter. But that's huge, Desi. And the fact that you never told me, leads me to wonder what else is going on here."

"What do you mean?"

"If the two of you knew each other, how the hell did she end up on the jury?"

"How should I know? It wasn't like I put her there."

"But you recognized her when you saw her in that courtroom."

Desi paused. "Yes," she murmured.

"Was she asked if she knew you during jury selection?"

Desi nodded, and then shook her head. "She said she didn't."

Now it was his turn to pause for thought.

Did he know? A chill slowly crept up her spine. The way he was looking at her . . . Desi wanted to tell him. Jesus! She wanted to tell him everything—going to see Mary, just to talk. She wanted to tell him about how all she wanted was to ask Mary Travis why she'd lied and said that she didn't know who Desi was when the attorneys asked her. He was so close to figuring it out. Desi could see it in the way he looked at her. Solomon was a smart man. It wouldn't be long before he put all the pieces together. Mary Travis was dead, and every confession she'd ever made had died with her. Would he believe them if they heard Mary's confessions come out of Desi's mouth? She knew better than to think that he would.

"What did you do, Desi?" he asked, gravely.

"Nothing!" she blurted out. An overwhelming rush of panic washed over her like heat. "You think I—"

He took a step in her direction. "I'm asking you to be honest with me," he coaxed.

Desi's heart sunk. She was going back to prison. All of a sudden she couldn't breathe.

"I'm not stupid, Desi," he continued, calmly. "I put puzzle pieces together for a living. The pieces of this one are coming together in a way I don't like. Mary had been your teacher. She sat on that jury that sent you to prison." Solomon slowly approached her.

Desi sat in the chair, unable to move. She couldn't breathe. The room was starting to spin as she realized why he'd come all this way. She couldn't go back! Dear God! She couldn't go back! But he knew. *Tell him! Just say it! Tell him!*

Desi could see their faces all over again. Every man and woman on that jury refused to look at her when they came back into that courtroom. The judge asked them if they'd reached a verdict and Mary stood up.

"*We have.*"

"*Madam Forewoman. How does the jury find?*"

"We find the defendant guilty, Your Honor."

When Mary Travis said those words, she looked right at Desi, like she didn't know her. She looked at Desi like the two of them had never sat on that woman's front porch drinking sweet tea together, while Miss Mary told Desi how important it was for her to do well in school so that she could get into a good college and make something of herself.

"Desi?"

Desi began to shake uncontrollably and glared at him. Not this time. She'd be damned if she let anybody do this to her again. "She fell," she whispered through tears.

She wasn't going back to prison!

"The paper said she fell." Desi defiantly glared up at him.

He stood there. "It did," he responded quietly.

Let him try to send her back to prison. Desi would fight him. She'd fight for her life this time, spending every dime of that money she'd inherited to pay some goddamned lawyer to kick some prosecutor's ass in that courtroom.

Desi rose to her feet and stepped toward him. "Why are you here?"

He remained as cool as a cucumber. "I had to know. I had to look into your eyes when we had this conversation."

Solomon had come all the way out here, playing his lawyer games, trying to push buttons and to get her to admit something that he'd only suspected.

Desi walked over to the door and held it open for him to leave. "Get the hell out of here!" she demanded, without looking at him.

She left the door open and walked away, turning her back to him.

Solomon didn't move.

She turned to him. She couldn't hold her tongue anymore. He was standing here, accusing her when his judgment should've been saved for his aunt.

"You think she was a saint?"

The look on his face told her that he didn't like the question.

"Desi, don't."

"Don't what?" She smirked. "Don't tell you the truth? Isn't that why you came here? She wrote me letters," Desi confessed. She'd never told anyone about those letters. Not her mother. Not even Lonnie. "The woman sent me to prison and then had the nerve to write to me, telling me about how sorry she was for what she had to do."

The confusion in his eyes almost made her feel sorry for him. He didn't believe her, and Desi needed desperately for him to believe her.

"I saved them, Solomon. Every last one, written by her hand to me." She pointed to herself.

His confusion turned to pain.

"Mary Travis was no saint, and nobody knows that better than me. She felt guilty. It ate her up and she tried to make it up to me by sending me letters! Like I cared!" Desi didn't even realize that she'd started crying. "She was still free and I wasn't because of her! And I'm supposed to give a damn about her being sorry?"

"Desi . . ." he tried to stop her.

"'Shut up, Desi!' Is that what you want me to do, Solomon?" She walked over to him and pointed her finger in his face. "I am sick and tired of shutting up! Now, I got plenty to say and I'll be damned this time if I don't!"

The two of them came to an impasse. Desi sat at the far end of the sofa with her feet curled underneath her, looking away away from Solomon.

He stood staring at the open door long after she'd asked him to leave. Desi had shut down. She wouldn't answer any more of his questions, and she knew that Solomon had to have had a million of them.

The woman was his aunt, his mother's sister. Of course he wanted to believe the best about her, but now he had to wrestle with Desi's version of who Mary Travis had been.

"I'd like to see those letters, Desi."

She wouldn't even look at him.

"I need to understand."

To hell with him and understanding, she thought bitterly. Why should she care if he ever understood when Desi didn't understand it either?

Eventually, Solomon did the only thing he could do. He picked up his bag and left. Desi took a long, deep breath when he did, and held it. For now at least, there was nothing for him to say. Nothing for him to do except to believe her . . . or not.

After he left, Desi called Lonnie. "He thinks I killed Mary Travis."

"He can think what he wants. He can't prove shit."

Cabo

Jordan took a chance and had a courier deliver a plane ticket to Cabo San Lucas to Lonnie at her office. He thought about following it up with a phone call, but decided against it, and showed up at the resort hotel not knowing if she would take him up on his offer, or leave him to spend the weekend alone in the ocean-view suite.

She didn't disappoint. "How'd you know that the way to a girl's heart was a weekend getaway at a lux resort on the beach?"

Jordan stood on the balcony, with his back to the door, smiling to himself, as Lonnie came up behind him, wrapped two gorgeous arms around his waist, and nuzzled herself against his back.

"Lucky guess?"

She moaned, and rested her head on his shoulder. "How about a brilliant one?"

The two of them stripped down to nothing and lay out on the lanai on the chaise making slow, languid love all afternoon. The sun seemed to shine a spotlight on the woman, and she bathed in it, soaked in it until her beautiful dark skin glistened like something magical. Jordan loved looking at her. Lonnie's parents were Nigerian, but Lonnie had been born in Omaha. Her career path had led her all over the world, but ultimately, for some strange reason, she'd decided to settle in Texas, which just didn't suit her. Places like this—exotic, warm, and tropical— fit her like a glove, and if he could pack her up and leave her here for his convenience, he'd do it in a heartbeat.

"I saw your pretty wife on the cover of *Texas Woman Magazine.*" Lonnie bit into a fresh piece of mango, and fed him the other half.

"I didn't fly you out here to talk about my wife," he said, dismissively.

No married man liked talking to his chick on the side about his wife, and vice versa, naturally. But Lonnie liked watching him squirm.

"She's breathtaking." Lonnie smiled.

Jordan grunted.

"The article said that she's starting her own fashion line. She sews?"

Jordan reached for his glass of wine, and sipped.

"I should change the subject?"

He looked at her. "Yes. You should."

"How's mom?"

Jordan still didn't answer.

"You're starting to make me wonder if all we have in common is sex. You don't want to talk about her either?"

"Not with you?"

Lonnie frowned. "Ouch! That stung. So, what you're trying to say is, I'm just the ass on the side and that I just need to lay back, spread 'em, and look pretty."

He smiled.

She didn't. Lonnie was surprised by how insulted she felt. Jordan had gotten his and was holding her captive here in Mexico. The pendulum had swung to his side and he was being smug about it, which pissed her off, the longer she stared at him.

"Claire's the trophy, Jordan. Don't make the mistake of getting the two of us confused."

He lay back, pulled his shades down over his eyes, and ignored her. Lonnie was livid. She drew back her hand, slapped him hard across the face, sending those expensive shades flying over the stucco wall. Jordan grabbed her by the wrist.

"What the fuck's wrong with you?"

Lonnie tried jerking away from him. "You're what's wrong with me! I'm not Claire, Jordan!" she screamed. "You don't own me! You get it because I choose to give it to you! Don't get it twisted!"

"I get it because I want it," he growled in her face. "Don't *you* get it twisted!"

Lonnie swung her free hand at him again, but he caught it before it could make contact, twisted both arms behind her back, and pulled her down on to his lap. Jordan's penis was rock hard.

Lonnie fought. She didn't want him and she wasn't about to let him take shit that didn't belong to him. She tried raising her knee to his chest, but Jordan blocked it with his elbow. With one hand, he clamped both of her wrists behind her. He wrapped his other arm around her waist, raised her up, and forced himself inside her.

"You're mistaken," he grunted. "I own this!"

Jordan pressed his lips to hers and forced his tongue into her mouth. Lonnie bit down hard on it, hard enough for him to cry out, but he didn't. Jordan's stare locked onto hers and dared her to bite it off. Lonnie drew blood. He grabbed her by the neck and squeezed until she couldn't breathe. Jordan drove in and out of her as deep as he could. Lonnie's eyes rolled back in their sockets, her head fell back, and moments before she started to black out, he came. Seconds later, so did she.

The sun was starting to set, and Lonnie gazed lazily out at the ocean views more satisfied than she'd ever been in her life. Blood had dried in the corner of her mouth. Lonnie finally gathered enough strength to talk.

"How's the tongue?" she asked, lazily.

Jordan made a smacking noise. "Sore. But I'll live."

She raised her head to look at him. "I loved it," she confessed.

He ran his hand over her head, stared deep into her eyes and smiled. "I love you."

The Rock Cried Out

"That's her? You know? The one that killed that old rich man!"

"Girl! You lying!"

"I swear to God that's her!"

Days and nights bled into each other in one long thread of time. Desi cried a lot, especially at night in her cell. During the day, she did whatever they told her to do without question, and it seemed to be enough.

"I want it clean in here, Green," one of the guards told her, leading Desi into the bathroom. "Clean enough to eat off the floors or you'll do it again. Understand?"

"Yes, ma'am," Desi said quietly.

"You've got four hours," she said, looking at her watch before leaving.

Work kept her mind occupied. Desi made small projects major ones, concentrating her efforts into the details. It made the time go by more quickly. It kept her from thinking about where she really was, if all she concentrated on was a toilet or a shower wall. Every line, every crack, every nook held her *full undivided attention until she lost herself in the effort. The next thing she knew, she'd be done, and soon it would be time to go to bed.*

"Desi? Is that your name?"

Desi looked up from scrubbing the floor around one of the toilets when she heard someone call her name. Three women stood in the doorway of the women's bathroom.

"Y'all need to use it?" *she asked, slowly standing up.*

One of them looked like a boy, she even talked like one, and she came over to where Desi stood, and reached out to touch Desi's hair.

"Pretty," *she said, smiling.*

"She young, Ike. I told you she was," *one of the other women said. Desi looked up at her and noticed a green inked tattoo scrawled across her neck that read* Da Fellaz. *The one standing in front of Desi had it too, but it was written on the inside of her arm.*

"They call you Desi?" *the woman asked again.*

She had heard about them. Da Fellaz liked girls. Desi's heart beat like a rabbit's. She nodded. She wanted to tell them that she didn't want any trouble and that she had to hurry up and get this bathroom cleaned before the guard came back. She wanted to tell them that she didn't belong here, but Desi was too afraid to say anything.

The woman smiled warmly. "My pretty girl."

She walked Desi backward until her back was up against the wall. She wasn't as tall as Desi, but she was thick. "They call me Ike," *she said, standing so close to Desi that she could feel the heat of the woman's breath against her face.* "You like Ike?"

Desi looked confused and she shrugged. One of the women laughed. The other just shook her head. Ike leaned in close and kissed Desi lightly on the lips. Desi shuddered, and squeezed her eyes shut. Ike laughed, and then backed away.

"*A virgin*," she chuckled. "*I ain't had me no virgin in years.*"

Desi reluctantly opened her eyes, and Ike blew her a kiss. "*Keep it sweet for me, baby girl!*" She winked then she and the others left. "*I'ma put my name on that 'fore it's all said and done.*"

For the next month, Desi did whatever she could to avoid running into Ike. But if Ike saw her first, Desi was at her mercy. Ike pinched, groped, kissed, and winked. She tortured Desi, promising to take possession of her, and Desi could barely eat or sleep for worrying about Ike. One morning in the shower, though, she realized that it wasn't Ike she should've been worried about.

Desi could feel Ike watching her, but she showered quickly, as usual. She slathered soap on her face, and when she rinsed it off, she saw Ike, standing in her stall, staring and smiling and licking her lips. Desi never even noticed the woman standing behind Ike.

"*Get it good, Elise,*" she heard someone say. "*Tear that shit up!*"

The woman scissored herself with Desi on the floor of the shower room, grunted like a man, then reached around to Desi's lower back and pulled and pushed against her, until she started to shudder, roll her back, and grunted.

"*Fuck! Ooooh! Fuck!*"

Minutes later, she shoved Desi away from her and fell backward onto on the floor the wet floor until she finally caught her breath and stood up. Desi curled up and cried.

The woman stood over her. "*I got that cherry,*" she said, glaring at everyone else. "*Who wants sloppy seconds?*"

"*Move!*" Ike called out, rushing over to Desi. "*I'm next!*"

As soon as Ike touched her ankle, Desi sat up and swung, landing a blow hard to the side of Ike's face.

"*Bitch!*" Ike spat, punching Desi so hard, she tasted blood.

Sue's mouth hung open in shock and amazement after listening to Desi recount her violent experience in prison not long after she'd gotten there.

"I—I—don't know what to say to that, Desi. I'm speechless."

"Then don't say anything," Desi said unemotionally, as if she were telling someone else's experience and not her own. "Just put it in the book."

"H-How did you manage to survive in that environment?"

"How did I survive?" She stared in astonishment at Sue. "You want me to tell you how many times I cried myself to sleep, or thought about killing myself, or how many times I prayed until my knees swelled up, begging God to get me out of that place only to realize one day, that He didn't listen to prayers from prison? Is that what you want to hear?"

Sue looked confused. "I don't understand."

"You're fascinated with this martyr shit, Sue. You can't get enough of it, but when it comes to writing about Billings and that mess he did, all of a sudden it's gossip, it's tabloid crap and not worthy of putting into your book."

"I thought we'd gotten past all that?" Sue said, irritably. "Is that how this collaboration is going to be? Adversarial? You against me?"

"Not if you cooperate." Desi smiled.

Sue frowned. "Meaning?"

"Meaning, you write what you like to write, and you write what you don't like to write. If it comes out of my mouth, then it goes in the book."

Sue thought about it for a few moments before responding. "Or else what?"

Desi defiantly folded her arms in front of her. "Or else, I'll keep the really juicy stuff to myself and maybe even sell it to some tabloid later on."

"That's low," Sue protested.

"Take it or leave it."

It took only a few seconds. "I'll take it."

To Protect and Serve

Retired Police Chief Thomas Billings had faithfully served this small community of Blink, Texas for more than forty years before retiring seven years ago. Residents of Blink referred to Billings with warm and heartfelt regards, using words like caring, thoughtful, and fair. But it seems that the chief of police had a dark side. Maybe it was his warm and caring nature that compelled him to help sneak desperate illegals across the border from Mexico into Texas. Perhaps he believed that he was helping people build better lives for themselves. Or perhaps, Tom Billings was driven by greed and power, transporting desperate and trusting people from one hell into another. As the FBI closed in on one of the largest human-trafficking organizations in the country, they soon realized that they were closing in on public officials, hired to uphold the law, to protect and to serve.

Desi had come across the article over the Internet, and it read verbatim to the e-mail Lonnie had sent her detailing the role Tom Billings was suspected to have played in a large human-trafficking ring. Lonnie's investigative reporter friend, D. Rohm, had followed up on a tip about Billings, and stumbled onto the biggest breaking story in his career.

When asked who his source had been, the man couldn't say. The tip had been anonymous. Desi soon learned that Judge Fleming's transgressions had been a part of a bigger picture that led D. Rohm to Billings.

"I'm not surprised," Lonnie said to Desi after the reporter told her of the connection. "Fleming and Billings lie together, probably share the same little country-ass brain. They ganged up on you together. Why wouldn't they be redneck deep in this shit together too?"

A Fevered Pitch

It was good to be home. As much as Sue loved New York, all the excitement and energy of that place wasn't beans compared to her quiet home in the northern Virginia suburb. Virginia had trees, plenty of them. And Sue had a thing for trees. Mornings were the best. Sue brought her cup of coffee with her outside to the porch and sat in the swing she'd insisted her husband, Evan, have installed. She wore a pair of his socks, some old sweats, and a tank top, then wrapped herself in one of his sweaters to ward off the chill of the morning air. The sun was just starting to come up. Sue took a deep breath, a sip of coffee, and slowly exhaled, doing her best to reenact one of those fresh coffee commercials where the woman looked so perfectly content and beautiful as she savored one of life's precious moments.

The soft creaking of the screen door snapped her out of her dreamy trance. "You're insane. You know that, don't you?"

Evan came out onto the porch and sat down next to her. He even had the audacity to take her cup of coffee from her. "Didn't we just go to bed?" he asked, irritably.

Sue chuckled and ran her hand through the wild salt-and-pepper spikes of hair on his head. "Just because I'm up, doesn't mean you have to be."

He grunted something inaudible, but she decided that he'd said something along the lines of, "I missed ya."

"Besides." She took her cup of coffee back. "I have a ton of work to do today."

"You always have a ton of work to do."

They had been together for twenty years, married for nine of those years. He'd put on at least twenty pounds since she'd first met him. Sue had put on . . . a few, which was all she'd ever own up to. His dark hair had turned gray. Sue hid her gray with a chemical compound that always equaled auburn and they were as comfortable together as a well-worn pair of shoes, but she still found him as sexy as the day she'd first laid eyes on him.

"I have a deadline," she said, simply.

"You always have a deadline."

"What time will you be home tonight?" she asked, feeling surprisingly aroused.

He looked at her. "Why? What do you have in mind?"

She smiled devilishly. "Handcuffs, blindfolds, and," she shrugged, "maybe some honey."

He cocked one thick, dark brow. "Honey too?"

"Unless you prefer whipped cream."

"No, honey's good. I like honey. It's sticky."

"I know, baby."

Evan placed a heavy hand on her thigh. "So . . . I could go in late."

"So . . . you could."

The two of them looked at each other, and suddenly bolted up from the swing, and raced each other inside and upstairs to the bedroom.

"I don't think we have any handcuffs, sweetie," he said, letting her pass him on the stairs.

"Socks!" she said, excitedly. "We can use socks!"

The sound of Desi Green's voice coming from that small recording was more haunting to Sue now than when she'd sat across from the woman in Manhattan. It filled Sue's office, the house, the block, and it reverberated off of her soul. Sue had expected Desi Green to be a walking heartache, wounded, a living, breathing tragedy, and a sad and lonely woman worth more than twenty million bucks. The reality was vastly different. Desi had had some heartbreaking years. She'd suffered more than most people, but the woman Sue had come to know was nobody's victim. And she wore that money of hers like the queen wore the crown jewels, as if it were her birthright.

"People think that if you're scared long enough, that all you are is scared, and that's all you'll ever be. And if you're not careful, you'll prove them right," Desi said, in her soft, Southern accent. "But eventually you get sick and tired of being afraid all the time. Fear is heavy, like carrying bricks around your neck all the time. That's not how I want to live the rest of my life. I've lost too much of it to waste it. Every day counts for me. Every minute. Every second."

"So you're not afraid anymore, Desi?"

Desi smiled. "Pay attention, Sue. I said no."

In 1985, eighteen-year-old Desdimona Green shot and killed million-aire Julian Gatewood in the living room of her mother's house. The young woman was sentenced to twenty-five years in prison for his mur-der. Six months after her release, she inherited twenty million dollars from her mother's estate, money left to her by the man her daughter murdered.

Sue pushed away from her keyboard, and stared at the words she'd typed on the screen, reading them over and over again, half a dozen times before finally typing her next, and most profound sentence. *Why did Desi kill Julian Gatewood?*

In all the years since Julian's death, no one had ever asked Desi that question. Sue hadn't asked it either because as much as she wanted to know the answer, Sue was terrified of it.

Sue stared long and hard at that question she'd typed on the screen, knowing that it was the only one that ever really mattered. It had been consuming Sue ever since she came across the saga of Desi Green.

"Are you going to tell me, Desi?" she murmured reflectively to her-self.

Sue's phone buzzed next to her indicating that she had a text. It was from Desi.

Tom Billings, the sheriff who arrested me, is dead.

Sue immediately dialed Desi's number to try and get more informa-tion, but got her voice mail instead. A few minutes later, she got another text from Desi.

He shot himself in the head. I shouldn't be feeling what I'm feeling.

Set Me Free

Desi was back in Texas, sitting next to Lonnie on her porch, looking across to the lake in front of her house.

"You know how many times I wished that man dead?" Desi had never admitted that out loud to anyone. But after her arrest, she had wanted Billings to die. "I prayed for him to be struck by lightning, or run over by a train."

"But now?"

"Killing himself, that was on his terms, Lonnie. He chose to do that, and he chose how he was going to do it."

"You got a beef with that?"

"How many people choose?" she asked, introspectively. "At the first sign of trouble, he opted out. He's a coward."

"The Billingses of the world are bullies. They can dish it out, but they can't take it."

"First Mary, and now him." Desi shook her head.

"I see a pattern emerging," Lonnie said, sarcastically.

"I never expected any of this." Desi said solemnly.

"What, Des?" Lonnie asked, irritably. "People die. Mary was old. Billings was a bitch."

"Mary died taking her confessions with her. Billings died with nobody knowing what he did to me. Nobody knows what either one of them did."

Lonnie looked at her. "You know."

"Yeah, but I'm the only one. Neither one of them made any grand speeches about how they wronged Desi Green. Nothing's changed. Mary Travis still walks on water, and Billings isn't the man everybody thought he was, but he still was the best sheriff Blink, Texas had ever seen."

"Is that what they're saying about it?"

"He's still the hometown hero," she said, sadly.

"Not to everybody, Des," Lonnie said.

"If even one person still thinks he is after all this, Lonnie, then that's one person too many."

Lonnie had been running her resources ragged trying and dig up dirt on Billings and Fleming, and for what? So, she exposed them as kidnappers and pedophiles? She hadn't been able to expose their involvement in Desi's trial and conviction.

"It'll all come to light when that book is published," Lonnie started to explain, sounding almost as if she'd read Desi's mind. "I've cracked the egg, Des. You're the one who has to pull it apart and expose the middle."

"I'll sound like I'm lying."

Lonnie shook her head, leaned forward in her chair, and covered Desi's hand with hers. "Open your eyes, girl. That's why I'm doing all this. When people see them for the kind of fools they really are, then they'll read what you say in that book differently. All of a sudden, you won't be the liar, Desi. People will give what you say credence, and they won't be so quick to discount your version of what happened because the reputations of men like these have been brought to light."

"I almost believe you."

"I believe what I'm saying. It's like building blocks. Without these secrets coming into the forefront, then it would be just your word against theirs. And your word would be crap next to theirs. But now." Lonnie smiled. "Desi, Billings isn't everybody's hero anymore. Fleming's reputation is about to go down the drain, and even Gatewood is going to feel the sting of what's coming his way."

"He's not old, Lonnie, and he's not weak like Billings and maybe even Fleming. Jordan won't put a bullet through his head to get out of this. He'll retaliate. We bring a stick to this fight, he'll come back with a bigger stick."

"How can you say that?" Lonnie looked perplexed. "Knowing what you know, how in the world can you sit here with a straight face and tell me that?"

"Because I know him. I know him, Lonnie, you don't. He will not go down without a fight, and honestly, his mean ass will probably win."

Lonnie looked at Desi and thought that she was a fool. If she believed that Jordan Gatewood could come through all this victorious and unscathed, after everything Desi knew, then she was a fool.

"Don't look at me like that, Lonnie," Desi blurted out. "You don't know him like I do."

"No," Lonnie wanted to tell her. "You don't know him like I do." But for now, she kept her mouth shut. For now, it was best.

While Desi was still pondering Tom Billings's suicide, Lonnie was reeling over her weekend in Mexico with Jordan and trying to make herself forget about that thing he'd said.

He'd said he loved her.

"That's not part of this equation, Jordan," she started to laugh.

He smiled. "I don't say things I don't mean, Lonnie."

She started to push up off of him, but he held her in place.

"I don't know what to do with that," she said.

"Just take it. I'm not asking for it back. It's something that's been building and I had to get it off my chest."

"What are you thinking about?" Desi asked her. "I can tell something's churning inside that head of yours."

Lonnie shook her head. "Nothing. Just the fact that Jordan Gatewood was trying to change the rules of their game."

No Woman, No Cry

"It's such a beautiful day," Olivia said, strolling around the lake on her property with her son.

It was a good day. A clear day. Olivia was present and aware and she enjoyed it fully.

"How about I take you to Strom's tonight for dinner?" Jordan asked, knowing that Strom's was his mother's favorite restaurant.

Olivia squeezed his arm, and gazed admiringly at him. "That would be lovely, Jordan. You know I haven't been there in a very long time."

"I know. And I'd love it if you'd accompany me."

"Yes, Mr. Gatewood. It would be my pleasure. I feel as if we haven't spoken in such a long time," Olivia said, earnestly.

"We speak every day, Mother," he gently explained.

A dark expression of confusion shadowed her face. "You know what I mean. How have you been, son?"

"I've been fine, Mother."

"Tell me you're not working too hard. How's Claire and when are the two of you going to make me some grandbabies?"

He chuckled. "We're working on it, Mother." It was a half truth. Claire wasn't on birth control. She hadn't been on any for years, and they hadn't even had so much as an "almost" pregnancy.

She scoffed at him. "Work harder," she commanded. "No offense, son, but you're not getting any younger."

"No, I'm certainly not getting any younger, Mother," he said, introspectively. Jordan had a daughter from his first marriage, Dawn, living in California with her mother, and attending UCLA where she was studying to become a doctor. Dawn was twenty-two, twenty-three years old by now. He'd broken her mother's heart, and she'd taken the baby and left him. It was one of those things that Olivia didn't always seem to remember, and one that he didn't see the need to remind her of now.

"Well, that wife of yours is surely young enough." Claire had just turned thirty-one. "She should be churning out children left and right, unless something's wrong with her."

He laughed. "There's nothing wrong with Claire."

Olivia's tone turned serious. "Then it's you," she said, sincerely. "Tell me it's not you, Jordan, but if it is," she hurried to add, "if it is, then these doctors today can work miracles, son. I can ask—"

"Mother," he interjected quickly. Talking to his mother about matters of sperm was downright uncomfortable. "I'm fine."

Olivia stopped walking. "Julian wanted so many grandchildren," she said sadly. A serene expression washed over her face. "He said he wanted a house full of them, laughing and playing, until they got on his nerves so bad that he could call up you or your sister to 'Come and get these damn kids!'" she mimicked him. "But I know," she said sadly, gazing out at the sunset. "I know you'd probably have had to get a restraining order to keep him away from his grandchildren."

The fact that she could still talk about his father with so much love for him, after what he'd done, amazed Jordan. For years he'd kept Ida Green set up in that house, in that small-ass town. For years he'd lied to Jordan's mother, telling her he was away on business, when in fact, he was an hour outside of town, laid up with that woman playing house.

"I know what you're thinking," his mother looked at him and smiled. "I can see it in your face. You're wondering how I could love him after everything that happened."

"You know me too well," he smiled back.

"It wasn't always like that, son. You only remember the bad parts because you were so young, and you're still angry with him."

"You should still be angry too, Mother."

"Holding a grudge won't change anything. And besides, I'm getting too old to bear the weight of regret." Olivia frowned. "Lord knows I've born more than enough. But sometimes, I give into it, the anger. Sometimes I hate Julian Gatewood as much as one human being can hate another, but never enough. Never completely."

"I needed him, Jordan," she said somberly, tears glistening in her eyes.

"Mother," he said, starting to interrupt. He didn't want to hear this. He didn't want her to punish herself like this over a man who didn't deserve her love.

"I know you don't understand, but I miss him, terribly."

"It's getting dark." He tugged gently on her elbow. "Let's go back to the house."

"You don't like hearing me say things like that." She looked at Jordan. "Do you?"

He was quiet for a moment, considering the best way to answer her question. "He didn't treat you right. That's what I don't like."

She shrugged and wrapped her arms tightly around herself. "Maybe he didn't. Maybe I didn't treat him so right either."

"Did you have a man on the side somewhere that we don't know about?" he asked flippantly.

"You're a grown man now, son. You're old enough to understand the complexities of relationships between men and women. Your father and I weren't a perfect couple, but we did love each other, Jordan."

He smiled politely. "Of course you did, Mother."

"But." She hesitated. "You don't believe he loved me. Do you?"

He turned to her and pressed her hand between both of his. "I believe that it's absolutely impossible for any man in his right mind not to love you."

Olivia stared suspiciously at him. "Your father was very much in his right mind, Jordan. Julian loved me in his way. And," sadness filled her eyes, "he loved her too."

Jordan's frustration shone through. "Julian was a fool and he made a big deal out of a woman that was no big deal."

"That's where you're wrong. He didn't make a fuss over her. Not like a man of his position should've."

His mother was talking nonsense, and he quickly concluded that she was losing her grasp on reality again. "He left her a fortune, Mother. I'd say he took pretty damn good care of her."

"He took more than he gave," she said, suddenly sounding bitter.

He studied her. "From her, or you?"

Olivia looked thoughtful for a moment. "Both," she said, introspectively. "We both sacrificed, and we both lost so much because we loved him. In his own way, he loved both of us, and if he could be condemned for anything, it was for being greedy, wanting to have his cake and eat it too. And—we let him."

"Ida Green can rot in hell for all I care, Mother."

"If she rots in hell then so will I," she said, with sadness filling her eyes.

Jordan stared warmly at his mother, and put his arm around her shoulder. "Julian was a fool," he said, resentfully.

She patted her son's hand. "We are all fools, son."

Olivia wore her favorite blue dress and the diamond teardrop earrings Julian had given her for their ten-year anniversary. Olivia hadn't been out of the house in such a long time and tonight, she was being escorted by one of the most handsome men in Dallas, her son.

The fine-looking man waiting for Olivia at the bottom of the stairs took her breath away in his dark suit and crisp white shirt. He looked so much like the man who sired him sometimes that it made her ache in-side. Olivia always believed that it made his father ache sometimes too.

He looked up at her and smiled. "Hello gorgeous," he said as if he meant it.

Olivia paused. He was such a mean and angry man. He had gone out of his way to try and hide his anger from her, but she was his mother. Of course she knew it was there—always. He hadn't always been that way. They'd turned him into the man he was now. Olivia and Julian had created the monster that was Jordan and they had been responsible for who he had become.

Overwhelming guilt threatened to swallow her whole at that mo-ment. "I'm sorry, Jordan," Olivia finally said with all of the sincerity she could muster.

He looked confused. "Mother?"

She loved him. Olivia loved her son now, more than ever. And she forgave him for the things he'd done, and for the things he would do in the future.

She pulled a warm and appreciative smile from someplace deep down inside her. "I'm starving," she said, reaching for his arm. "If I don't get some food in me soon, I'm liable to take a bite out of this big, strong arm of yours." She squeezed him.

He laughed. "You don't want to bite that," he teased. "It's tough and sinewy."

"Just like your old momma." She laughed.

Contrary Mary

Desi sat stoically across from Solomon in his office, waiting while he read through half a dozen of the letters Mary had written to her through the years. The first letter was dated nearly a year after Desi had been incarcerated.

Dear Desi,

I don't expect that you'll even open this letter, let alone read it after you realize who I am, but I pray that you will. That's all I can do—pray. Lately, I've found myself praying more for you than for myself and hope that God is listening and watching over you. If he is listening to me, then I believe he will answer, if he knows that my thoughts are solely with you in that prison.

I am as convicted as you are, but for me there will never be a release. I am condemned to live out the rest of my life here in this miserable body, but that's as it should be.

You will be free someday. I believe this. I know it. And when that happens, maybe then I can rest.

Truly and sincerely,

Mary

In the first few letters, spread years apart, Mary appeared to be begging for Desi's forgiveness, but later, their tone changed, and she focused more on "her girls" as she called them, young and troubled girls in high school that she mentored and became somewhat of a surrogate mother to.

The graduation ceremony was lovely. Mariah looked so beautiful and so proud of herself. She wants to teach, like me. Of course, I am so hopeful for her. I told her that she'll have to work hard, but that I would help her in any way that I could. Thankfully, the community college here doesn't cost as much as a four-year university, but I told her that she can start here, and later, apply to school to finish getting her bachelor's degree. Mariah is so patient and smart that I know she'll make a great teacher, and helping her to achieve her goal is more of a blessing to me than it is to her.

Thank you, Desi.

Truly and sincerely,

Mary

After he finished reading, Solomon looked up at Desi. "Did you ever write back?"

Desi shook her head. "I never did."

"So, why keep them?"

She shrugged.

"Why do you think she wrote them?" he asked, but Solomon was sure that he already knew the answer.

"Guilty conscience."

Mary had been guilt ridden over sending a young girl to prison. Jurors felt guilty all the time. But Solomon had been quietly putting the pieces together in his own mind, and he didn't like the picture they'd created. She'd used her own money to pay college tuition for several teenage girls, money that seemed to come when she needed it.

One of my girls, Brandy, was so upset when her mother put her out after finding out that she was pregnant. How could a mother, a good mother, turn her back on her child when she needs her the most? Brandy had nowhere to go, and no job. But I managed to find her an apartment of her own near a good school and across the street from a nice park. She was happy, but was so worried that she couldn't pay me back the year's rent I paid for it. I didn't want her to pay me back, Desi. That money is doing some good for people who need it. It's not mine. It never was.

"Do you think she took money, Desi?" he managed to ask, nearly choking on the question. He needed to hear it from somebody else. He needed confirmation that he wasn't just jumping to an ugly conclusion about a woman he loved dearly.

"I do, Solomon," she said, softly.

His gazed locked onto hers. "Why do you think she'd do something like that?"

"You're asking me?"

Solomon's heart sunk to his stomach. If the Gatewoods wanted to ensure a conviction, then all they had to do was buy one. Desi had been young, pretty, and it was possible that a jury would've felt enough sympathy for her to possibly find her not guilty. Maybe, they didn't want to risk it.

"I am sorry for your loss, Solomon," Desi finally said. "The loss of your Aunt Mary, and the loss of the faith you once had in her. But I'd be lying if I said that I gave a damn about her," she said, bluntly. "If she thought she was doing me any favors by helping those other girls, then she was wrong."

"People make mistakes, Desi. You should know that better than anybody."

"Some mistakes you can't recover from or make right. I do know *that* better than anybody."

Solomon handed her back her letters. Desi took them and left.

He didn't have the heart to share what he'd learned about Mary with his family. Obviously, Mary had made some mistakes in her life. And what was even more obvious—she regretted them.

Solomon sat in his office long after everyone else in the firm had left for the day.

A member of a jury trial had been bribed. How many more had been paid? How many sold their pleas for a price? One question led to another and another until it had snowballed to a monstrous proportion. All of a sudden, what had been so clear cut and dry, wasn't. And if Mary Travis was no longer what he and so many others had believed her to have been all these years, who else involved in that trial was hiding behind a mask?

Desi's perfume lingered in the air after she'd left. It was as soft and as understated as she was. Solomon had judged her and convicted her like so many others. She had every right to hate him. She had a right to hate all of them.

Sue Me

With Desi back in Texas and Sue back at her home in Virginia, the two had started collaborating over the Internet, using video chat.

"When you first told me about Tom Billings, I felt it would make you look vindictive, which would lessen the impact of your story," Sue explained. "I thought it would turn the book into more of a soap opera than a memoir."

Desi surprised her and laughed. "It is a soap opera, Sue."

"No, Desi. If anything, it's even more tragic than I thought it could be."

"Don't get depressed on me, Sue Parker."

"I'm not depressed. I'm angry. This ordeal with Billings raises a lot of questions for me, questions that I never thought to consider before."

"Like what?"

"What kind of law officer could he have been when he was capable of something so horrific?"

If she expected Desi to answer that question, Sue was disappointed. Desi had no answers.

"He had no integrity," Sue said. "How can anyone ever trust any arrest he made, any decision he made?"

Again, Desi was silent.

"He wasn't a good man, so therefore, how could he have been a good cop? He couldn't have treated you fairly, Desi," she murmured.

"No," Desi finally spoke, "he couldn't have."

Sue took a deep breath, held it, then released it slowly. "Why did you kill Julian, Desi?"

Desi pressed her lips together and then blinked away tears. "I never said that I did."

A big, old rock found its way into Sue's stomach, as she recalled video footage of Sheriff Billings being interviewed when news of the trial went national.

"Sheriff, can you speculate as to why or how this happened?"

"It's hard to say what goes on in the minds of young girls," he said in this thick, Texas drawl. Billings adjusted his cowboy hat.

"Based on your report, things probably aren't looking good for Desi Green."

The reporter shoved the microphone back under his nose. He shrugged. "I'm not here to speculate, son, but—well, that's for a jury to decide."

All sorts of wild ideas began to run through Sue's head. "You were convicted of murder, Desi. A jury says that you were guilty. I need to know why you did it."

"'You're a smart girl, Desi.'" Desi started to repeat things told to her after her arrest. "'Don't say anything.' 'Let your lawyer speak on your behalf.'"

"Desi?"

"'Be a big girl for Momma. They'll turn what you say around and make it sound like you confessed.'"

Sue's heart broke. "Aw—Desi."

"Money talks, Sue. I didn't shoot Mr. J. Why would I? I loved him." She bit down on her bottom lip before making the confession that would shake Sue to the core. "He was my father."

"You mean he was like a father to you," Sue asked for clarity.

"He was my father, Sue."

After that revelation, Desi had to suddenly get off the computer. Sue sat stunned, shaking her head. Was it true? Was Julian Gatewood really her father? There'd never been any mention from any media outlet that Julian was Desi's father. Was she making it up? Obviously, Desi Green was full of surprises and so much more complicated than Sue could've imagined. And this story—this story was turning into something messy, something Sue had never expected.

Sue's phone rang and Jeremy's name popped up as the caller.

Sue groaned. "Yes," she said, wearily.

"Stop the presses," he blurted out.

She was still in shock from Desi's revelation. "What?"

"Literally," he said, dryly. "We've been slapped with an injunction order from Gatewood. We've been ordered by the courts to stop all action regarding this book."

"Are you serious?" she asked, stunned.

"Very."

Sue sighed, and rolled her eyes. "Fuck!" she murmured.

Jeremy surprised her and laughed. "You know, until this moment, I believed that I'd let you talk me into making the biggest mistake of my career."

Sue thought the man had gone mad. "And now you don't?"

"Sweetheart." He laughed even more. "Jordan Gatewood has just sold the first hundred thousand copies of this book for us. All of a sudden, Sue Parker, people are going to give a damn about Desi Green more than I ever thought they would."

"So, this is a good thing?" she asked, sitting up straight.

"It's fabulous. Hurry up and get me that story."

"But I thought you said—"

"Since when have you ever listened to a word I've said?"

Do I Move You?

Her mother was buried out here. It felt strange coming back to Blink to attend Tom Billings's funeral when she didn't go to Ida's, but ever since she'd seen on the news that he was dead, Desi had been—she'd been— She didn't know how she felt. Just all of a sudden, a piece of the puzzle that had been her past was gone and she had to see it for herself. She had to see them put him in the ground.

"Why'd you shoot him, Desi? Why'd you shoot that man?"

Tom Billings, Sheriff Tom Billings, was as tall as Julian, white, with a face that always looked old, even when he was younger. Heavy lines were etched deep across his forehead and around his mouth and eyes. She remembered his hands, big and crooked hands, long fingers with big knuckles.

"You had the gun. You had the gun in your hand, Desi! I saw you! Unless you think I'm blind or something. Is that it? You think I can't see what's right in front of my face?"

"I—I—don't—"

"I ain't in the mood for your lies, girl! I got a dead man in that morgue at the hospital!" Cold, black eyes drilled into her, warning her that he didn't believe her and that nothing she said was going to change his mind. *"He's dead because of you, and you're gonna pay for this, Desi. I guarantee you. You're gonna pay for this."*

Desi slowed the car down and pulled into a space along the curb behind one of the limos. She'd gone to the church where they had his ceremony. And she'd had every intention of going inside, but Desi waited outside in the car. She couldn't bring herself to walk into that church. They said nice things about people at funerals. The last thing she wanted was to hear nice things said about Tom Billings.

The crowd was four or five deep around the grave site. Desi walked slowly, shutting out the sounds of whispers and stares of everyone around her, fixing her gaze on the coffin that held him inside. Tom Billings had shot himself. He'd put a forty-five underneath his chin and pulled the trigger. People parted and let her through. They knew who she was. Voices floated past her like clouds and time seemed to nearly stop as she stood there next to his coffin and watched them slowly begin to lower it into the ground.

Desi held her breath the whole time. The people here loved Tom Billings. He was their friend, family member, colleague. They admired him, and trusted him because he was, after all, hired to serve and protect them. He kept them safe. Arrested bad guys—and girls. These were the people who didn't believe what they'd read in the paper about him or saw on the evening news. These were the people who would go to their graves believing that Tom Billings was every bit as good as he'd wanted them to believe.

Tom Billings was a criminal. He took women and children and sold them off to whoever had enough money to buy them. And he didn't care what happened to them. He didn't care that they might be abused, or mistreated. He didn't care that they might be raped or killed. They were burying their good friend, their loved one, but they had no idea who he really was. Desi had no idea either. Back then, when he took her to jail, she believed what they all believed. That he was one of the good guys.

Russ Fleming could hardly believe his eyes. Desi Green stood on the other side of Tom's coffin, looking nothing at all like that crying teenager he'd remembered. Wearing a simple fitted black dress and shoes, she wore her hair pulled back away from her face and dark sunglasses.

"What's she doing here?" his wife whispered, leaning over.

Tom had been convinced that Desi had sent that letter in the mail to him. Russ thought he was crazy for even thinking something as outlandish as that, but now—seeing her here—he couldn't help but wonder if Tom was right.

She stayed until Tom was put into the ground, and then Desi Green raised her chin and stared across at Russ. He couldn't see her eyes on him, because of the shades, but he felt them. Slowly, she turned around, and walked back the way she came.

Jesus! What had she done? And more importantly, what was she planning on doing next?

A Rich
Tale A Rich
Tale

False Friends

Seeing Jordan Gatewood in the papers or on the news was one thing, but seeing him in person was something else altogether. The man really was larger and more intimidating in person. Russ hadn't seen him up close since he'd convicted Desi. Back then, he wasn't much more than a boy, trying to be a man. He looked as scared as shit back then. Jordan had suddenly inherited a kingdom, and he had some big shoes to fill. Russ remembered feeling almost sorry for him and the challenge that lay ahead of him. And just like everyone else, he expected that boy to fall on his ass and lose everything his father had worked so hard to build. He'd surprised Russ. Hell, he'd surprised everybody.

You don't call a man like Jordan directly and ask for a meeting. You especially don't call him if the only thing he knows about you is that you took money from his attorneys to cover up the truth of his daddy's murder. Russ Fleming was nobody to the Gatewoods. But *Judge* Russ

Fleming had saved their reputation, their image. He'd done it for a price, though, a high one. Tom Billings had done his part as well.

Jordan refused to come to Blink, and he refused to allow Russ to meet with him at his home or in his Dallas office. They met in a small town thirty miles south of Ft. Worth called Lochner, a sleepy little town with a population of about twenty-five thousand. Russ waited inside the bar at a table next to the window, nursing a cold beer when Jordan pulled up in an old pickup truck. He stepped out of it wearing worn jeans, cowboy boots, and a hat. It was hard to downplay greatness, though. Russ watched the big man walk from the dirt-packed parking lot to the door. He listened to the long, heavy stride of Jordan carrying across the wooden floors to Russ. He was surprised that Jordan recognized him.

He sat down without saying hello. Russ let a nervous smile escape and regretted it as soon as it did. It was obvious from the look on Gatewood's face that he resented being asked to take this meeting. But he'd come anyway. Maybe history had compelled him. Maybe curiosity. Maybe a little bit of both. Dark, hooded eyes bore holes into Russ.

"You heard the news about Tom Billings."

Tom Billings could've died and been buried as quietly as most men, but the story that broke in the papers the day after he died changed all that.

"Apparently, he wasn't the man everybody thought he was," Jordan responded unemotionally.

Russ was smart enough to read Gatewood's expression. Tom Billings and whatever illegal activities he was involved in had nothing to do with him, and Russ had better have a more compelling reason for calling this meeting than to talk about Tom Billings.

Russ nervously gulped down some of his drink. "He uh . . ." He took a deep breath before continuing. "He called me the night he . . ." Russ darted a glance at Jordan. "He hadn't been involved in any of that mess for years!" he growled.

"What do you want?" Jordan asked abruptly.

Russ had been going over the last conversation he'd had with Tom in his mind since the sound of the gunshot went off in his ear over the phone. Tom had been babbling about nothing—at least, that's what Russ thought that night. But the more he thought about it, and after seeing Desi show up at that funeral, he had no choice but to think that Tom was probably on to something.

"Desi Green showed up at Tom's funeral," he said.

Something changed in Gatewood's face.

"The day he died, he told me that somebody had found out about— what he'd been involved in . . ." His voice trailed off. "They had contacted him, sent him things in the mail." Russ shrugged. "Evidence?"

He'd managed to get Gatewood's undivided attention all of a sudden. "He thought it might've had something to do with her."

"How?"

Russ swallowed, and shrugged his shoulders. "I have no idea," he said dismally. "I didn't think much of it. Just thought he was being paranoid." He looked over at Jordan again. "Or feeling guilty. But when I saw her the other day," he explained nervously, "there was something about her being there, almost as if she was there to make sure he wasn't getting up."

Silence loomed between them for several minutes before Jordan finally spoke. "Why'd you call me, Fleming?"

Russ raked his hand across his graying hair. "I've gotten some things sent to me," he admitted reluctantly.

"What things?"

Russ waved his hand dismissively. "It's not important."

"It must be important, Judge," Jordan interjected. "Whatever it was that Billings received was important enough for the man to put a bullet in his head. Billings believed Desi Green had dug deep enough to find his dirtiest laundry. You believe she's done the same thing to you?"

Russ blinked anxiously. "I don't know! I don't know, but her showing up there like that after the conversation I had with that man the night he shot himself can't be a coincidence! I don't believe in coincidences! Not like that!"

"Why the hell did you call me?" Jordan asked, threateningly. "What do you think I'm supposed to do about any of this?"

"Have you gotten anything? Anything at all, something strange or something related to the trial, maybe?" Russ asked, pleading for answers from Jordan. "Or am I just a crazy, paranoid old man like Tom was? If he was right . . ." His voice cracked. "If I'm right, then—she needs to be stopped, Jordan."

"You've wasted my afternoon." Jordan sighed.

"Is she making us pay for what we did, Jordan?" He reached across the table and desperately grabbed hold of Jordan's arm. "She's got the money! Tom believed she was behind this!"

Jordan jerked his arm away and gritted his teeth. "Whatever you and Billings have done, Judge, that's for you to make peace with."

"You paid us!"

Jordan glared at him. "I've never given you a dime!"

"But your attorneys did!"

Jordan reached across the table and grabbed the older man by the throat. "I'm not my attorneys. Whatever you and Billings did twenty-five years ago had nothing to do with me. If you think I'm wrong, then prove it. You call me when you do."

Russ turned a violent shade of red, and gasped for air, until Jordan let go, stood up, and marched out of the place.

Mr. Backlash

"*What are you doing* here? Do you know what time it is?"

It was after ten at night, and Solomon had shown up at her door uninvited.

"I need to talk to you."

"Then call me, first."

Solomon stepped inside, again, without waiting for an invitation.

"What's your problem, Solomon?"

"Tom Billings," was all he said.

Desi threw her arms up in frustration. "Oh, what? You think I killed him too? What about JFK or Martin Luther King, Jr.? Maybe I knocked both of them off during recess."

"He was the cop who arrested you."

She folded her arms defensively, and stared angrily at him.

"Now he's dead? First Mary, and now Tom?"

"I'm getting tired of this."

"I'm trying to get to the bottom of it."

"It? What—it? The bottom of what?"

"Of what happened to you!"

His outburst caught her off guard. "You know what happened to me," she said calmly.

"I have my suspicions," he responded. "And if I'm right . . ."

"If you're right . . . what?"

"I'm an officer of the court, Desi." He sounded almost as if he resented that fact. "And I'm obligated to report this so that an investigation can begin."

"What kind of investigation?"

"An investigation into your arrest, your trial. If any procedures weren't probably adhered to, then . . ."

"Then I get my twenty-five years back? I get my mother back, my youth? Can I go to the prom now, Solomon? Can I fall in love, get married, and have babies?"

Solomon looked helpless, as helpless as she'd always felt.

"No. I guess not." She answered those questions for him.

"You'd get a chance to clear your name, Desi."

Desi laughed. "Well, I guess that's something."

"Or would you just rather see everybody dead?"

"I didn't do anything to those people," she repeated wearily.

"Well, how can you explain what's happened?"

"Maybe it's God," she said flippantly. "Maybe God really don't like ugly, and he's decided to finally do something about it. Maybe it's just—a coincidence. And maybe it was just Aunt Mary's and Uncle Tom's time to go," she snapped.

"You think this is funny?"

"No." She shook her head. "But yeah. I kind of do, because you're so concerned about those two people biting the dust, Solomon. She took bribes for her guilty vote, and he bought and sold people like cattle, and you're standing here in my living room all broken up about them. I think that's hilarious."

"And what if I told you that you were wrong," he said, coolly. "What if I told you that it's you I'm all broken up over? Would that still be funny?"

Desi wiped the smile off of her face. "Comical."

"Why?" he asked, taking a cautious step toward her.

Desi stepped back. "Because I wouldn't believe you."

He stepped closer again. "Why not?"

This time, she stood her ground.

He took another step. He'd tried not to think about her, but lately, thinking about her was all he could do. Desi the murderer. Desi the liar. Desi the victim. Desi's perfume, her lips, her hair.

"You can't just come here and think that we're going to . . ."

"We should."

I don't know you," she protested, weakly.

"You can."

"You have no idea what I'm capable of," she murmured.

"I think you're wrong. I think I do."

"You should be afraid."

He stood close to her now. Too close. Solomon loomed over her, pressed his nose into her hair, and inhaled.

"What are you doing?"

"Getting to know you," he whispered, closing his eyes and inhaling her hair again.

Desi shuddered unexpectedly. "I'm not in the mood for this, Solomon," she forced herself to say. "I swear I'm not." Desi raised her hands to his chest and leaned into him.

He raised one hand to her waist, until his palm rested on her spine, and pulled her close. Desi tried to pull away, she wanted to resist, but—. Solomon wrapped both arms around her, and pulled her to him, held her, until she melted against him.

He hated what he believed to be true. He hated knowing that the legal system had been manipulated at the expense of a teenage girl, and that greed had taken over, and that those same people who were supposed to take care of her had all betrayed her. Mary Travis and Tom Billings had finally paid a hefty price for their transgressions. But there were others he suspected had been bought off too: Robert Chen, another juror, who disappeared six months after Desi was sentenced and Barbara Ciades, who died of a heart attack ten years ago, behind the wheel of her 1987 Mercedes. She'd been a waitress at a local diner who didn't even make minimum wage. Phillip Atkins, the defense attorney, had moved out of the country a month after Desi's conviction.

The Gatewoods had bought and paid for a guilty verdict, and they'd gotten their money's worth. Maybe they'd hoped she'd die in prison, but Desi surprised them, and not only did she survive, she came out a very rich and beautiful woman. The irony was a mother fucker.

That sound of a beating heart was the most soothing sound in the world, and his was strong, steady, and deep. Desi closed her eyes and kept her ear pressed to it. The two of them stood there, rocking slowly back and forth.

"You finally have furniture."

Dammit! Why'd he have to talk?

"Finally."

"Where's the bed?"

His question wasn't lost in translation. She reluctantly pulled her ear from his chest and looked up at him.

Solomon shrugged. "Or I could just stand here all night and hold you."

"Foreplay with you is pure brain stimulation, Desi. Makes me rock hard."

She laughed. "You're kind of scary."

He shook his head. "Between the two of us, you're scarier than me."

But Desi was nervous. Her first love had been a prison guard named Jorge Vega, who claimed to love her, until she found him loving a few other inmates too, and that had been years ago.

He started backing her up toward the staircase.

"It's been awhile for me," she said, clearing her throat. "It's been awhile."

He raised an eyebrow. "How long's awhile?"

"Don't worry about it," she quickly shot back. "You married?"

"Divorced."

"Girlfriend?"

"No. Not—no." Solomon leaned down and picked her up. "Where's that bed?"

Her breasts were beautiful. Her ass was beautiful. Her back, stomach, legs—forty-four years and every inch of it was perfect. He kissed the soles of her feet, only to discover that she was ticklish. He kissed the center of her pussy, and discovered that she was eager. Solomon licked the tips of her nipples and found her responsive, and when he put his tongue in her mouth, he discovered that she was delicious.

He sat on the side of the bed with her perched on his lap, easing slowly in and out of her, holding her by the waist as she leaned back and rolled her hips in small circles, their gazes locked onto each other. He pulled her in closer. Desi wrapped both arms around his neck, and held on as he slowly raised and lowered her down onto his shaft.

"I like that," she whispered in his ear. "Don't stop."

He liked it too. Hell, he loved it.

She let go of him and pressed soft lips against his. Desi eased her tongue into his mouth to the rhythm of their lovemaking. She let her eyes close, let her head fall back, and arched her back. Ripe, dark nipples jutted up at him, and Solomon pulled her close again, took hold of her breast, and pulled it into his mouth.

Desi moaned, rolled wider circles in his lap, and began to buck wildly.

He didn't know if she was cumming or just enjoying the moment, but he smiled.

"One Enemy Is Too Much"

—*George Herbert*

Jordan had always enjoyed the hunt so much more than capturing his prize. He'd courted Claire until she had no choice but to fall in love with him, but he'd never loved her. Lonnie was not Claire.

She stood on the outside patio of his St. Regis penthouse, overlooking the city. The two of them had taken his private jet here for dinner, with plans to fly back in the morning. Jordan studied her from behind, knowing full well that she was much more impressed by the views than she ever was with him.

"I can feel those eyes of yours burning a hole my back," she said over her shoulder. "It's rude to stare, Gatewood."

"I could give a damn about being rude."

She was his match, so much more than Claire ever could be. Lonnie was not swayed by money or luxuries. She had her own. She had a career that she was proud of, independence that she clung to fiercely, and she didn't need him.

Lonnie turned around and walk over to him, took his martini from his hand, finished it, and then handed him back the empty glass. "Wow," she said, licking her lips. "That was good. Can you make me another one of those?"

He bowed slightly. "It would be my pleasure."

Jordan went back over to the bar.

"This place is swanky, Jordan. I dig it."

She kicked off her pumps and stretched out on the sofa. "You come here often?"

"Not often enough. Maybe," he said, looking at her, "that'll change."

Lonnie suddenly laughed. "Oh, I see how it is. You want to hide me out up here in the tower like Rapunzel?"

"She had hair, but that's not a bad idea."

"As nice as this place is, you know I'm not the type to be kept."

Jordan came over and handed her a freshly made martini.

Lonnie smiled. "Oooh! Nice and dirty. Just the way I like it."

Jordan came around, raised her legs up off the sofa, and then laid them across his lap again when he sat down.

"I don't want to lose you," he said, abruptly.

Lonnie grimaced. "Don't start Jordan," she complained.

He laughed. "I told you. I never say anything I don't mean."

"Look, I'm trying to be nice to you."

He cocked an eyebrow. "Trying to be nice to me?"

"Jordan, I'm not the marrying kind. And plus, you're already married."

"So, then what's the problem? I'm not expecting us to change anything. I'm married and I've been seeing you on the side."

"The side is good. But it gets all messed up when you toss around words like 'love' and phrases like 'I don't want to lose you.' We don't need to complicate things."

"But I do love you, and I don't want to lose you."

"How could you possibly love me when you have no idea who I am?"

"I know what I need to know."

"You know what I let you know."

Jordan grinned. "Is that a challenge?"

"No, man!" Lonnie sat down her drink, crawled across the sofa and straddled his lap. She cradled his face in her hands and stared into his eyes. "Don't mess up a good thing, Jordan. Don't love me. Don't try to own me. And don't ever try to boss me."

"You like it I when take control."

"No I don't."

"You came like a freaking maniac the last time I did."

"I faked it."

"You nearly fainted."

"I couldn't breathe. You were killing me."

"Your words, 'I loved it.'"

"And I lied."

Jordan held on tight to her and stood up. Lonnie clamped her legs around his waist.

"Oh, so now you're going to toss me over the ledge?"

"Nah," he said, kissing her lips. "We're going swimming."

"Don't you want to take your clothes off first?"

Jordan stepped down into the pool, shoes and all. "Too late."

"This dress is expensive."

"I'll buy you another one."

"You ain't buying me shit. I buy my own clothes."

"Okay."

"I didn't mean that."

"I know."

Lonnie watched him sleep. The bastard had gone and changed the rules on her and she had no idea how he'd done it. Love wasn't something that she'd avoided. It just never fit anywhere in her life. Lonnie never had the time for it, or the patience. Not that she loved Jordan, but he was making a big push to change her mind. She liked him, though. That much she could admit. Lately, he'd seemed to leave his asshole tendencies at the door. Lonnie almost felt guilty about following through with her plans. Almost, but not quite. She'd made a promise to herself on Desi's behalf. These people, these Gatewoods, had turned that woman's life upside down. That's the part she had to hold on to. Jordan could be a monster, a bully when he chose to be. That fact hadn't changed no matter how sweet he was to her now.

"What's wrong, baby?" he asked, groggily, turning over on his side, and draping his arm over her. Jordan kissed her sweetly on her head. "Can't sleep?"

"No."

She didn't even know if he'd heard her, before he drifted off again. Lonnie nuzzled closer to him, pressing her head against his chest, she inhaled deeply, and savored his scent. He smelled good. But didn't he always?

The Night I Fell in Love

Russ wasn't a fag. This boy, and other boys like him that he'd been with were fags. They knew it, and they were proud and easy with what they were, strutting around the club, switching like girls, chattering like them, and batting their eyelashes like them. He liked what they did to him, and how they did it, with no rules or reservations. They did things his wife wouldn't dare do to him. Things she'd slap him across the face for if he'd even hinted that he wanted her to try.

He wasn't a pervert, either. None of his boys was ever much younger than eighteen. They were grown men, young, but grown, and consenting. He never forced himself on any of them.

Toby was one of his favorites. A petite boy with a long torso, short, shaggy hair, and full, soft lips, Toby lived to please. He loved sex, and he loved to talk. Some of the others were mechanical, just following along, doing whatever you told them to do. Toby didn't resent spending time with Russ, and he always seemed genuinely happy to see him, whether Russ was there for him or someone else. Toby always greeted him with a hug and a kiss.

"I'm getting old," he pouted, patting Russ's lapels. "You haven't asked for me in months, so it must mean I'm getting too old."

Russ chuckled, and patted Toby's behind. "You're being silly. You know you're my favorite."

Toby raised a shy gaze to meet his. "Then how come you haven't asked for me?"

"Ah, sweetheart." He sighed. "There're a lot of new faces here. I'm just sampling."

"The young ones are taking all the attention."

"Now, you know I don't spend time with anyone too young," Russ reminded him. "I'm just—experimenting. It's my way of making sure I don't get too serious over anybody."

Toby blushed. "By anybody, do you mean—me?"

Toby was too pretty to be a man. And he played this role better than any woman Russ had ever met. He'd had affairs with women before. The magic came and went too quickly. The fantasy faded almost as quickly as it started. With Toby and the others, the fantasy was all that mattered, and they took it and ran with it. That's what kept Russ coming back time and time again. It never got old, or predictable. It was as if everyone who walked through those doors understood that reality had to be checked with their hats and coats.

"Of course I mean you." Russ's heart skipped a beat. The pretty lover he held in his arms cast a spell over him once again. "You'll steal my heart if I'm not careful," he said, daring to go a little further down the rabbit hole.

Toby smiled warmly. "Then you go and play with the other boys," he said sweetly. He pulled free of Russ's grip. "I'll be here when you're ready to come home." He winked, and blew Russ a kiss as he turned and walked away.

Aaron was new here, a slender black lad with the most beautiful mouth

Russ had ever seen or tasted. He watched in awe as nineteen-year-old Aaron sucked and slurped patiently on his cock. Russ sat on the side of the bed in the private room, running his hand across Aaron's hair, smiling appreciatively down at him.

"That's it," he said, over and over again. "Take your time," he told him. "There's no rush."

He wasn't an old man here. And the routine that had become his life was nothing but a figment of his imagination in this place. The moments were special, the encounters—memorable. The sex, mind-boggling. It was his little piece of heaven.

Heat crawled up the back of his neck, and beads of sweat erupted across his forehead. Russ Fleming stared in horror at the photograph he held in his hands. He let his eyes close, and let his thoughts drift back to a moment he'd wished had never happened.

He didn't look like the same young man Russ had spent time with that night. Aaron Baker. That was the name in the small newspaper clipping that had been in the envelope with the photograph.

He slid his reading glasses up to the bridge of his nose, and read through the article from a newspaper from a small town in Louisiana.

FIFTEEN-YEAR-OLD MISSING

was the headline. He'd told Russ that he was nineteen. Russ swallowed.

Aaron Baker was reported missing six months ago by his grandmother, Lois Baker. He was a freshman at Smith High School. Aaron is five-nine, weighs one hundred and fifty pounds, and was last seen getting into a black pickup truck outside of his high school.

There was nothing else in the package delivered to Russ's house. He'd closed himself off in his home office and had been there for hours wondering how this could've come to him.

He and Aaron hadn't spoken to each other in front of anyone. They'd made eye contact across the room. Russ was intrigued by the young man. All it took was a nod indicating that he would like to get to know Aaron better in private. He led the way down a corridor to the private rooms. Aaron followed and the two of them . . .

"Supper's ready, Russ," his wife called to him from downstairs.

A guttural groan escaped from the back of his throat. Russ hadn't meant to go as far as he did that night. Other club members told stories, but he'd never even come close to entertaining the thought of—

"You can do what you want here," he'd been told. "What happens here stays inside these walls. We take care of each other."

"Russ?" His wife opened the door without knocking.

"Dammit, Delilah!" he spat angrily.

She looked stunned. "It's time to eat," she said, surprised by his outburst.

"I'll be down shortly," he said, struggling to compose himself.

"What's wrong with you?" Delilah stepped into the room and walked toward his desk.

Russ tossed a book on top of the picture lying on his desk. "Nothing," he grunted. "I'll be down in a minute, honey." He forced a smile.

Delilah sighed, tossed a hand up, and turned to leave. "I ain't keeping it warm," she said irritably, slamming the door behind her.

The only people who knew anything about Aaron Baker were club members. The longer he sat there and began to put all the pieces together, the more obvious it became that it had to be someone from the club who had sent this garbage to him. Someone from the club or . . . Desi Green.

"Four-four-five-seven-six," he said to the person on the other end of the phone. "I need a meeting." Russ pulled out his handkerchief and swiped it hard across his forehead. "Immediately," he said gruffly, before hanging up.

He'd paid those people too much money to have his confidence betrayed like this. And if they were behind this shit, if they were the ones who'd taken that picture with some kind of plan to try and extort something from him, or if they had sold it to her to use against him, every last one of them would be sorry as hell. Russ was a small-town judge, but he wasn't one to be messed with. His connections went further than the city limits of Blink, Texas. They went all the way up the ladder to the Texas Supreme Court, and if these mother fuckers wanted to dance, then he'd snatch the goddamned lead right out from under them.

To Feel Again

She came here more often that anyone knew. Olivia knelt at Julian's headstone, laying a spray of golden irises at the base of the marble headstone.

JULIAN ADDISON GATEWOOD

1936–1985

Every man dies. Not every man really lives

—WILLIAM WALLACE

Every time Olivia came here, she left overwhelmed by sadness and grief. She turned and looked over her shoulder at her driver leaning against the car, waiting patiently for her. Olivia seldom left the house anymore, except to come here. She turned back to Julian's headstone with tears in her eyes and watched it dissolve into a moment from her past.

"*Charles,*" *she said to her driver from the backseat of the car.* "*Promise me that you won't tell him about this.*"

She had hardly ever said two words to that man before, but tonight, for whatever reason, he seemed like the only friend she'd ever had in the world.

"*Yes, ma'am.*" *He looked back at her from the rearview mirror.* "*I mean, no, ma'am. I won't mention it.*"

The children were safe at home. God, how she loved her children, Jordan who was headstrong and determined like his father, and Janelle, her quiet and timid princess. She lived for them, and her family meant everything to her. Olivia would do anything to keep them together.

Charles parked the car out in front of a house so small, it reminded her of a box made of bricks.

"*How could he stand such a place?*" *she asked herself in a whisper.*

There were no immediate neighbors. The house seemed even smaller because of the distance from the others. She walked up the sidewalk and noticed the silver sedan parked in the driveway. The air smelled of honeysuckle, and fireflies flitted around her, seeming to light her way.

Olivia turned to look over her shoulder at her driver, leaning against the car, waiting patiently for her. His presence reassured her.

A woman knows when her husband is being unfaithful. She'd come to confront that other woman, and to bring her husband home.

"*Jesus!*" *Ida ran, stumbling out of that house, moments after Olivia had arrived.* "*She shot him! Dear God! She shot him!*"

The faint sounds of Olivia's own voice echoed in her mind. "*No!*" *she cried as she cradled her husband's head against her chest.* "*No! Julian!*"

The room filled with a kaleidoscope of colors, movement, and sound.

Charles rushed in from outside. "*Oh, Lord!*" *He rushed over to Olivia.*

"Mrs. Gatewood. Put him down," he told her. "Put him down and come with me."

"No! No!" Olivia shook her head violently. She held on tighter to her husband.

She didn't remember leaving Julian, or walking down the stairs of the porch. Charles poured her into the backseat of that car. Olivia looked out of the window and saw Ida collapsed to her knees on the grass, crying uncontrollably.

Charles disappeared back inside that house, came running back toward the car, piled into the front seat behind the steering wheel, and shot out of that town like a rocket.

The void Julian had left behind was gaping and endless. Olivia had felt cold inside since the day he'd died.

"Mrs. Gatewood?" Her driver came up behind her and gently helped her to her feet. "It's getting late, ma'am." He smiled. "I need to get you home."

Olivia looked up at him, confused. He looked like . . . "Charles?" she asked, her voice trembling.

He smiled. "Not Charles, ma'am. I'm Paul. His son."

He helped Olivia into the back of the car, and slowly pulled away from the curb. She remembered Desi's face. Olivia had barely even noticed that the girl was in the room when she walked into Ida's house. It wasn't until the trial began, and she saw who was being charged with Julian's murder that she saw what Desi looked like. She looked like a child, fragile and afraid.

"Testify? There's no way my mother is up to testifying!"

"The only other witness is Ida Green, and she's going to lie to protect her daughter! Now, if you don't want her to get off, Jordan . . ."

"*I don't!*"

"*We can't guarantee it. Not without Olivia's testimony.*"

Olivia never testified, and yet Desi Green was found guilty. Olivia guessed they'd found a way to make sure of it."

Waiting for a Surprise

The unidentified body of a young, black male was found early this morning by a hunter, deep in the woods of Pearsall, Texas, an area popular for hunting whitetail deer, wild hogs, and fishing. The body was reportedly discovered wrapped in tarp material, and was buried in a shallow grave, found by the dog of the visiting hunter. Authorities report that the remains were badly decomposed, and that they are hoping fingerprints or dental records can help identify the victim. No word yet on cause of death.

The automated voice on the other end of the phone prompted Russ for his ID number. "Four-four-five-seven-six," he responded nervously, swallowing the bile that had risen in the back of his throat.

"Yes," a man responded mechanically.

"I was assured that the matter was handled." He spoke quickly.

The voice on the other end was quiet for several beats before finally responding. "It was."

"Is that— On the news. They found someone." His hands shook so hard, he couldn't control them.

"I assure you," the man continued in monotone. "All precautions were taken."

Rage washed over him like a hot wind. "What the fuck does that mean?"

"Calm down."

"Have you seen the fuckin' news?" he shot back, angrily.

"Yes."

Russ waited for the man to elaborate, but he didn't. "Is it him?"

Again, the man was in no hurry to respond.

"Well?"

"Yes."

He sunk deeper into his chair. "Oh, God!"

"All precautions have been taken," he repeated.

Russ abruptly hung up on him. The boy had tried to take pictures. He'd had Russ in his mouth when Russ saw the camera hidden on a shelf across the room behind one of the plants. The red light caught his attention.

"What is that?" he asked.

"Don't you like this?" The boy looked up at Russ. "Don't you like me?"

The steady red light hypnotized him, and Russ pushed the younger man aside and crossed the room. He stared full-faced into the lens of a video camera.

Russ turned to the other man. "You put this here." His heart raced. Heat washed over his face. Russ's palms began to sweat.

"No! Of course I didn't put that there!" He stood up, yelling. But Russ knew

he was lying. He could tell when people lied. Hell! He'd made his living look-ing at and listening to liars!

"You put this here," Russ said again, holding the camera in his hands, and stepping toward him.

His face twisted in anguish. Liars looked like liars. Russ could almost hear the wheels spinning in that boy's head as he searched for a way to get out of this.

"Why would I do that?" he argued. "Come on, man," he said, pleading with his eyes. "We were having a great time. Just—throw it away. Break it or something! Let's finish what we was doing."

Russ had placed all his trust in this place. He had believed that he was safer here than he was in his own home. He had put his trust into these people, and most of all, into this other man. He'd trusted him with his most intimate self and desires. He had been gentle and caring with these people. He had been kind and generous, and patient. Russ had had the patience of Job with some of these men. He began to wonder—how many other cameras had caught im-ages of him naked? How many others had lied to him, betrayed him in this place? Everyone was searched when they walked through those doors. Even elite members, like Russ Fleming were searched for cameras, weapons, anything that could cause harm to another individual. Everyone trusted that their secrets would be well-kept here.

"How'd you get it in here?" he asked, stalking the other man until he backed him into the wall.

He shrugged. "I didn't! I swear I didn't!"

"How'd you get this past security?" Russ yelled, his eyes wide and wild.

He was on that camera. Russ didn't have to see the footage to know it. It had been running since he'd walked into that room. It was running as he got undressed. It was running when he kissed the other man. It was running when he sat down on the side of that bed.

"I didn't, man! I didn't even know it was there!"

But he lied. And it was a lie that sliced into Russ like a dull blade. He hit him. Russ hadn't planned to, but it happened. He hit him with that video camera, in his head, in his face, over and over again. He hit him until blood spattered the walls, the crisp white linen on the bed, and Russ. He hit him until he stopped begging Russ not to.

Oh, Sinner Man

After he left Cabo, Jordan kept himself busy, avoiding his wife. He hadn't seen Claire in over a week. She was sitting in the living room with another woman flipping through pages of fabric swatches when he walked into the house.

"May I take your bag, Mr. Gatewood?" the maid asked.

"Hey baby!" Claire exclaimed, bolting to her feet and rushing across the room to greet him. She wrapped both arms around his neck and kissed him. "I didn't think you were getting in until tonight."

"Change of plans," he said dryly.

She looked radiant, fresh, and genuinely happy to see him. "We'll be wrapping up shortly," she said so that the other woman couldn't hear her. "I need to get reacquainted with my husband."

Jordan excused himself and went upstairs to the bedroom, undressed, and took a shower. He stood there, letting the water wash over him, thinking about Cabo, Lonnie, and what he'd said to her. Jordan was so engrossed in his thoughts that he never even heard the bathroom door open. The next thing he knew, Claire walked up behind him in the shower and pressed her naked body against his back.

"I've missed you so much," she murmured, resting her head between his shoulder blades.

Jordan couldn't help himself. He became aroused, turned to her, and raised her chin until her lips met his, kissing her in a way he hadn't kissed her in years. Claire moaned, and dug her nails into his back. Jordan bent low enough to grab her by the thighs from behind, raised her up and pressed her against the wall, parting her legs and pushing deep inside her.

He closed his eyes and when he did, it wasn't Claire that he was making love to. What in the hell was wrong with him. Jordan forced images of Lonnie into his thoughts. They were her thighs he held in his hands, her tongue he tasted, her breasts brushing against his chest.

"Baby," she whispered, her breath grazing his ear. "I missed you , so much." Lonnie wrapped her lips around his. "I love you."

Jordan opened his eyes. Claire was caught up in the rapture of him. He felt nothing.

Claire thrust her hips forward. Jordan moaned, and forced himself not to lose his erection, but she wasn't the one he wanted, not even enough to fake it.

Claire opened her beautiful amber eyes. "What's—What is it?" she asked, desperate to keep that shower action going. "Jordan? Baby?"

Claire wasn't what he needed, and Lonnie was playing games. Jordan pulled out of his wife and carefully lowered her to the floor. He turned his back to her, picked up the bar of soap from the soap dish and started to bathe.

"I need to finish my shower, Claire."

Jordan didn't actually see the humiliation on her face, but he felt it. Claire left as quietly as she had come in.

He found Claire sitting on the side of the bed with her back to him when he came out of the bathroom.

"You must be serious about this one," she said, without turning around. "To shoot me down right in the middle of fucking me." She turned to look at him. "Must be love," she finished sarcastically.

Jordan ignored her, and pulled a pair of boxers from the dresser drawer. He spotted a half-empty bottle of bourbon on the nightstand on her side of the bed.

"How long have you been seeing this one?"

"Don't start."

"I'm not the one who started this, Jordan," she said, casually. "You did. And then, once again, you didn't follow through."

"Have you eaten? Drinking on an empty stomach can make you sick, wife."

"Like you give a damn."

"Obviously, it gives you a false sense of courage, too. Makes you say the kind of shit you'd know better than to say sober."

"Oh, I say it all the time, Jordan, sober, drunk. Just not always loud enough for you to hear me." Claire had started to cry. He wasn't surprised. Drunks cried.

"I'm so tired of living like this. Why do we have to keep doing this, Jordan?"

Jordan sighed irritably, stood up, and slipped into his robe. "Come downstairs. I'll make us both a sandwich."

The phone on the small table next to him rang.

"Jordan," the man on the other end of the phone said before Jordan could finish saying hello. It was Alan Spectrum, the prosecuting attorney at Desi Green's trial. "Fleming's been arrested."

Jordan was caught off guard by the statement. "Russ Fleming?"

"One and the same."

"For what?"

"Believe it or not, murder."

He had just seen Fleming recently and the man was sitting on pins and needles, concerned about his buddy's suicide.

Jordan's mind split into half a dozen different pieces, as he tried to make sense out of all of this.

"Who do they think he killed?"

"Some kid." Spectrum sighed. "Turns out the judge has a thing for teenage boys."

Jordan was speechless, as it all started to come together in his mind.

"Something's going on," Alan continued. "I thought it was all just coincidence, but— First Mary Travis dies. She was sick, and sick people die. So, I didn't think much about it."

"And then Billings," Jordan muttered.

"It still could've just been a coincidence in my mind. The fact that the crap he was involved in somehow became public knowledge—I shrugged it off too. But with this, with Fleming being pulled into the mix too, Jordan, there aren't that many coincidences in the world."

He was right. Tin soldiers were dropping like flies, and it all pointed to one menacing conclusion.

"The only common denominator between these people is Desi," Alan concluded. "Somehow, someway, she's involved, Jordan. I'd bet my paycheck on it."

Jordan hung up and went downstairs. All of a sudden, he'd lost his appetite. No matter how many different angles you tried looking at it, every line pointed back to Desi. Maybe she'd hired some fancy investigator or computer whiz to hack into private networks. Desi had gone out and bought a brain with some of that money of hers. And one by one, she was coming after everybody she thought had ever done her wrong. Sounded like the lyrics to a damn country and western song. She'd made one mistake, though. Desi had saved Jordan for last.

Some Discarded Valentine

What was she doing? Desi finished putting her lipstick on, and stared back at herself in the mirror. In the last week, Desi had spent nearly every one of those days sexing Solomon, talking to him over the phone, or wishing she were sexing him, or talking to him over the phone. Russ Fleming had been arrested for the suspected murder of a young boy. Another of Lonnie's "contacts" had somehow discovered the undiscoverable.

"I need to know who you know, Lonnie, and how do they manage to find out shit like this when nobody else can?"

Lonnie laughed. "It's all about knowing what you're looking for, Des, or in this case, *at*. All I did was focus my efforts onto your judge and your sheriff. Look long and hard enough at anybody, and you can find what they don't want you to."

"You ever look long and hard at me?" Desi asked, hesitantly.

"No, sweetie. You're an open book. I never had to."

Desi could hear Lonnie take a bite out of an apple, "I gotta go. We need to do lunch. It's been a while."

She hung up before Desi could say good-bye.

Solomon hadn't asked her about the judge, but the issue hung heavy between the two of them, like he knew she'd played some part in what was happening to Judge Fleming.

Desi was playing with fire. She hadn't killed Tom Billings, or Mary Travis, but she was still guilty of arming them both with the tools to kill themselves, and she'd stood by and done nothing to stop them. Could she go to prison for that? Guilty by omission? Did that apply to her?

Every fiber in her being warned her against spending too much time with Solomon, but those same fibers had been hella lonely for a long time. She hadn't known how much she'd needed to be with someone until he came along. But she couldn't afford to let her guard down. He hadn't come out and said it, but she knew that he wasn't 100 percent convinced that he should be spending all that time with her either. He didn't fully trust her. She could sense it. And she couldn't blame him.

Desi was leaving soon for North Carolina to work with that writer, Sue Parker. A night out on the town had been his idea. Desi had casually mentioned to him that she'd never been on a real date before, so he felt obliged to take her out.

He couldn't help but smile when she answered the door. Desi had let her hair down, and cascading curls fell to her shoulders. The dress was black, fitted, and teased him with delicious-looking cleavage. She bottomed out with red stiletto slingbacks.

"Wow!" he said, examining her from head to foot. "You look beautiful, baby."

Her smile made his day. "Thanks, Solomon."

He'd already seen her naked, but seeing her dressed like this made her brand new to him all over again. He admired the view from behind as they made their way to his car. Once settled in, Desi asked him to reveal the secret plans he'd made for the evening.

"So, where are we going?" she asked, reservedly.

"Well, I thought we'd start off with bowling." He glanced at her, and was slain with a disapproving look.

"Do I look like I'm dressed for bowling?"

"No, you do not," he said appreciatively, staring at her like she was his next meal.

"So, where are we really going?"

"Dinner and dancing," he announced.

"Dinner I can do, but," she paused, "I can't dance."

He started the car. "Well, then we'd better get started so I can teach you how to boogaloo!"

Desi just looked at him.

She was a horrible dancer, but she looked damn good doing it. Solomon danced circles around Desi, who seemed to have mastered the art of the two-step, but to add even one more step would've been a problem. She laughed as he spun around her. Blushed when he took hold of her hands and pulled her close. She stumbled when he tried to spin her, but whenever he pulled her near, and held her, Desi melted.

It was one of those old-fashioned, "keep your girl close" kind of dates. He held her hand when they weren't dancing, and couldn't take his eyes off of her when they were. She loved every minute of it. Desi let her guard down, she pulled back the layers of the stigma that had been hers for so long, and let herself swim in the idea that she was normal. No one in the room pointed a finger and said, "Look, that's her. That's Desi Green!" And she didn't stand up on top of a table and announce it either.

He led her back to their table and flagged down the waitress to bring them two more drinks.

"Having fun?" he asked, leaning over to talk in her ear above the music.

Desi nodded. "I'm having a blast."

It showed. She was the most beautiful woman in the room as far as he was concerned, and he knew that it had more to do with the radiance coming from the inside than anything she could've put on.

Solomon leaned in, put his hand under her chin, and turned her face to his. He kissed her, and smiled.

Russ Fleming had been taken into custody for the murder of a fifteen-year-old boy. Solomon had spent the better part of the day trying not to connect Desi to it, but he'd failed. First Mary. He didn't have any evidence, nor did he want any that his aunt had taken a bribe to make sure Desi Green was convicted. Then there was Tom Billings, the good-ol'-boy sheriff of Blink, who'd arrested Desi, and who, by his testimony, had seen her holding the gun when he and his men entered the residence the night Julian was killed. And now Russ Fleming, the judge who had sentenced her, was being held on capital murder charges. There was just something not all the way right with this picture. One by one, those who had trespassed against Desi were falling. But what right did she have to destroy them, when she was the one who shot and killed a man?

Desi smiled and winked a pretty brown eye at him as she took a sip of her drink. "If you still want to go bowling, I'm game." She shrugged.

Against his better judgment, he had gone into full and complete sucker mode for this woman. It clouded his thinking, made him look past the obvious or make excuses for it, and ignore the doubt gouging his gut.

"And if you give me a kiss right now, I might even let you win." Desi closed her eyes and puckered her lips.

Solomon couldn't resist.

Obeah Woman

"I thought I told you to hold off, Lonnie!" Desi said angrily over the phone. She was sitting at the airport waiting for her flight to board when she saw a small clipping in the *Dallas Morning News* about Russ Fleming's arrest.

"I decided that it wasn't in your best interest to wait," Lonnie said, coolly.

"If you gave a damn about my best interest, you would've listened to me. We're moving too fast. I wanted you to hold off with Fleming until after Sue and I finished with the book," Desi argued. "Leave some space between him and Billings. How long do you think it's going to take the media or the police to see the pattern here? How long do you think it's going to take for all of this shit to point back at me?"

Lonnie had betrayed her. She'd blatantly disregarded Desi's concerns and went ahead and did what she wanted to do.

"And what if they do, Desi?" Lonnie asked, calmly.

"Mary Travis fell and hit her head."

"I know. I was there. Remember?"

"Did you push her? Trip her? Pick up that table and bash her over the head with it?"

"You know I didn't."

"Did you put that gun in Tom Billings's mouth and pull the trigger?"

"Alright," Desi said, agitated.

"Did you hang out with that old perv and fondle little boys or bash their . . ."

"Alright!" Desi shouted. "I hear you. What am I going to do if the police start investigating me? And you know they will."

"What did you think was going to happen when that book was published? Did you not think that you were going to have to face the music at all, Desi?"

"No, I didn't."

"What difference does it make? And what reason would the police have for investigating you for any of this? These people fucked up. They cast the first stone when they were guilty as hell in their own right. This is just good, old-fashioned karma hard at work."

Lonnie's argument was on the money, but Desi still couldn't help feeling queasy about Fleming's garbage being made public on the heels of Billings's.

"You think you're being so brave by writing a book," Lonnie continued. "You think you're taking a stand, but I think you're all smoke and mirrors, Des. You talk a good talk, but when it comes to walking the walk, you're still that scared kid these people bullied into submission."

"Shut up, Lonnie." Desi snapped. "You keep saying that you're the one putting your ass on the line, but it's my ass they're going to be look-ing at to connect all of this to."

"What difference does it make if the world finds out about Fleming now or a year from now? He did what he did, and he has to pay for it."

"They're going to blame me—"

"Telling your writer the truth about these people is just a step, Des. A small one. Letting that publisher print the truth in a book is another step. But it's passive-aggressive behavior at best. These people aren't afraid of your book, Desi. It's your word against theirs. But none of them can argue the evidence, the facts. So, when your book is published, it's your word against the words of slave traders, child killers, and bribe takers. I promise that your word will stand on its own when it's all said and done because of what I've done for you."

"I'm glad you're my friend and not my enemy, Lonnie."

"You should be."

Desi could be her own worst enemy sometimes, Lonnie concluded after hanging up the phone. She was big on intentions, small on nerve. She liked to think she'd finally grown into that big girl who wasn't afraid of the boogeyman anymore, but she wasn't fooling Lonnie. Lonnie had taken the ball and ran with it. All Desi had to do was sit back, and let her. Now she was panicking, afraid that the fallout from Lonnie's dis-coveries about Billings and Fleming would draw too much attention to her, but attention was something she should've been used to by now. And whether that attention came today, or a year and a half from now when her book hit the shelves, well, she'd just have to deal with it. But at least, the truth about those bastards would be out, and maybe Desi could finally find her vindication somewhere in the debris.

"Why do I care so much?" Lonnie muttered, raking her hand across her short hair.

Why did she care? Why was she working so hard to see that men like Billings and Fleming were finally held accountable for their crimes? Why had she sacrificed her time and her energy, digging through the trash to find dirt on these people? Because Desi couldn't—or wouldn't. And because it needed to be done, and Lonnie knew how to do it. She had spent years exposing secrets with her camera lens and reporting, and she had come to expect that everyone, especially those in power, had something to hide. Desi needed a champion, and Lonnie had volunteered for the job the day she first decided to write to Desi in prison.

"You want me to use that same song that I used last time?"

Cole was young, gifted, beautiful, and black. He was eager to please Lonnie. She'd met him while taking photos for another journalist writing a piece on inner-city underground hackers. They were the lost boys (and girls) of the cyber world, who hadn't earned fancy college degrees, or in most cases, high school diplomas. They were the ones who flew underneath the radar, and had mastered the art of computing, taking it to a whole other level and selling their services like crack dealers.

Cole Masters was a genius who'd even been hired by the occasional corporation to hack into corporate files of competitors. He'd been responsible for writing and planting viruses that took down social Web sites, and had even spread a complicated Trojan Horse that shut down an entire cell phone company, costing the business millions, and making the other company, the one hired to fix the problems, a fortune.

He refused to have his picture taken by Lonnie, because he was the only one still in operation. Cole Masters wasn't even his real name. The boy was brilliant, and he had a crush on Lonnie.

"Yeah." She nodded. "I like that song. I think it really drives the point home. Did you scan the pictures?"

"Yep," he said, typing feverishly on his computer.

Cole had an entire room dedicated for his work, filled with monitors, half a dozen computers, routers, and only God knew what else.

"What's the message?"

Lonnie thought for a moment, before finally responding. This had to be good, because Jordan wasn't uncomfortable enough. "Ashes. Ashes. They all fall down."

She'd come too far in this to stop now. Compulsion drove her to see this thing through to the end with Jordan. *For Desi,* she kept telling herself. Until recently, she'd believed that that was the reason for everything she was doing but lately Lonnie had had the nerve to be honest with herself, and to admit some cold hard facts. She loved the chaos. She relished the drama, and as far as Jordan was concerned, she welcomed the challenge.

For Lonnie, it had always been about proving that she could, and with a man like him, a powerful confident man, Lonnie had to prove even more. She had to prove that she wasn't the kind of woman to fall under his spell, like so many before her had. Jordan's reputation was legendary. Before and after his wife, he had been known for how well he gave chase, only to discard women like debris later. Jordan was ruthless. Lonnie was just like him in that respect. And there was no way she could let a little thing like love get in the way of winning.

I See You Crystal Clear

News of Fleming's arrest had gone viral over the Internet, a small-town judge arrested for murder in the same town where a retired sheriff had recently committed suicide after being exposed as a member of a human-trafficking ring. Authorities believed that the two men had more in common than just being associates. They were trying to link the trafficking of young boys to an exclusive underground network of pedophiles. The source of both stories was linked to a reporter named D. Rohm.

First Mary and Billings, and now Fleming? Obviously, Desi's goal was to topple an empire. Mary had taken a bribe for making sure that Desi was found guilty by that jury. Solomon had managed to get his hands on the transcript of that trial, and read Billings's testimony when he was called to the stand.

"I was the first officer on the scene," he explained.

"And what did you see when you arrived?" the prosector asked him.

"I saw Ida Green crouched down on her knees in the front yard, crying uncontrollably. I told my deputy to tend to her."

"You went inside the house?"

"Yes sir. The screen door was wide open, and I pulled my weapon and entered the premises. That's when I saw a man lying on the floor, his head in a woman's lap, and another young woman sitting on the couch holding a weapon in her hands."

Why would Ida Green leave her daughter alone in that house with a dead man and obviously the woman with Julian was Olivia. Solomon scratched his head. Even if she was upset, it didn't make sense to Solomon that Ida would run out of the house when Julian was shot, unless she felt threatened or was running to find help.

He continued reading, looking for testimony from anyone as to why Julian was shot. There was none. He looked for some explanation of why his wife was there.

Things got really interesting when he came across Ida's testimony.

"What was your relationship to Julian Gatewood?" the defense lawyer asked.

"He was my—my man."

"And how long had the two of you been in a relationship?"

"I can't remember."

How could she not remember? Solomon expected the attorney to ask the same question, but he didn't. He missed an opportunity and went on to the next question.

"Did Desi and Julian get along?"

She must've nodded.

"You have to answer the question out loud, Ms. Green."

"Yes. They got along fine."

"Were they getting along that night? The night he was killed?"

"I suppose."

Again, she could've elaborated. He could've made her elaborate, but he skipped over that opportunity like he had done with the last one.

"Is Desi a good student?"

"Yes. She is. Does all her homework, and I never have any problems with her."

"Thank you, Ms. Green. I have no further questions, Your Honor."

What the fuck? Solomon was more than perplexed by the account of testimony from Ida Green and by the behavior of the defense. It made no sense. The man failed miserably on so many levels that Solomon had lost count. He didn't push Ida for more information about the night in question, her romantic relationship with Julian, or the events leading up to Julian's murder.

The transcript of the prosecution's cross-examination painted a decidedly stronger position, delving deeper into the relationship Ida and Julian had, and pulling more detail from her about the events leading up his death. But the part of the transcript that struck Solomon the hardest were the last two sentences.

"Did you see Desi point the gun at Julian Gatewood?"

"I—don't know."

A copy of Ida Green's official statement had been filed along with that transcript. In her statement, she wrote that Desi and Julian argued a lot. She noted that Julian was more of a father figure to Desi, and oftentimes would try and tell her what to do. That night, the two of them had argued about Desi wanting to go to a party. He told her that she couldn't go, and she disappeared to her room. Moments later, she came back with the forty-five her mother kept under her mattress, pointed it at Julian, and pulled the trigger.

I know she didn't mean to do it, Ida's statement concluded.

Ida had seen Desi shoot Julian. Maybe she lied on the stand to try and protect her daughter, but her testimony was weak on both sides, and she certainly didn't appear to be going out of her way to help Desi's case at all.

It was all slowly but surely starting to come together in his head. Someone had paid Mary Travis a small fortune to make sure that the jury came back with a guilty verdict. If they bought Mary, then chances were good that they'd bought and paid for Billings and Fleming to make sure she didn't get off too. But Desi's mother? That's the pill that he had the hardest time trying to swallow. Her testimony did nothing to try and convince a jury that Desi was innocent. Ida had done just about everything she could to say as little as possible. But why? No matter how many ways he tried to look at it, the same conclusion kept coming back to him, twenty million dollars.

Forbidden Fruit

Olivia was having a dream, one that she couldn't wake up from no matter how badly she wanted to.

"Get the hell off my property!"

"Open the door, Ida! Let me in! Please let me in!"

"Get away from my door!"

"I can keep them from killing her, Ida! I'm the only one who can!"

All Olivia could hear was the sound of the wind, blowing past her. She listened for birds but couldn't hear even one of them singing from the trees. Sorrow carried thick across the breeze, brushing against her skin, leaving behind a sticky residue. And just when she had given up and was about to turn around and leave, Ida unlocked the front door, opened it just a bit, and walked away from it. Olivia cautiously let herself in.

The first thing she saw was the bloodstained carpet. She turned her head to where Ida stood, and stared at her, confused. Why in the world hadn't she cleaned it up? Why would she just leave it there like that?

She wasn't very pretty. Ida Green was small with big, wide eyes, and a mane of thick hair sitting wild on her head. She wore a baggy men's sweatsuit, two sizes too big.

"I told them what you did!" Ida blurted out. "Told them every damn thing!" Olivia walked toward her, and for every step she took forward, Ida took one back. "They think my baby did this! They think Desi shot him!"

"You told them she didn't?"

"Damn right, Olivia!" she shouted defiantly. "Damn right I told!"

A lump swelled in Olivia's throat. "Then how come I'm not in custody?"

Naturally, Ida had no answers. How could she?

"Why are you here?" Ida asked, bitterly.

Olivia had started to shake. No one knew she'd come here, not the attorneys, not her children. They all believed that Olivia was beside herself with grief, that she was fragile and falling apart, and she was, but not over Julian's death. She was all of those things over his life, this part of his life, with Ida and Desi, but strangely relieved now that he was dead.

After taking a good long look at Ida, Olivia scanned the room, still amazed that a man of Julian's stature could ever be happy in this place. If he loved Ida, why hadn't he bought her a bigger house? She lowered her gaze and fixed her sights on the dirty carpet.

"It doesn't seem like he's gone," Olivia said, softly. "Does it?"

If Ida heard her, she didn't respond.

Olivia turned to her again. "Do you miss him?"

Ida's face twisted in confusion. "What the hell are you doing here, Olivia?"

"Desi?" Olivia tried to smile. "Pretty name."

"H-How could you do that to her?" Ida asked, quivering.

"How could you do what you did, Ida?" Olivia's voice cracked. "Julian was my husband. My husband! Not yours!" She pointed her finger to her own chest. "He married me! Not you!"

"*Punish me then, Olivia! But don't make her pay for my mistake!*"

Olivia drew back her shoulders, and stood looking down her nose at Ida. "*It's out of my hands, now,*" *she said, defiantly.*

"*You have everything to do with it! Go to the police! Tell them what really happened. Tell them that you pulled the trigger. You shot Julian!*"

"*It's not that simple,*" *she said, quietly.*

Ida wiped away her tears. "*I got about six reporters that are gonna be in my front yard in the morning. If the sheriff won't listen to me, then I'll tell them what really happened.*"

"*If you're lucky, somebody'll believe you. If they don't, though, then you should say a long, hard prayer for Desi.*"

"*They'll let her go when I tell them what happened.*"

"*You could be right.*" *Olivia swallowed.* "*Or, they may just see what I see; a mother who loves her child and will do or say anything to get her off. No one else will accept that I shot him, Ida. Not the sheriff, my driver—no one. It would be your word against mine, and I guarantee you that yours can't possibly hold the same weight as mine.*"

"*I know you don't expect me to just sit here and not do anything! My baby doesn't belong in jail, and she doesn't deserve to go to prison over something you did!*"

"*The world isn't always fair. Consider this her first real lesson.*"

"*I won't let you take my daughter!*"

"*You took my husband!*" *Olivia lost control and cried.* "*My life!*" *She felt her knees grow week, and struggled to continue standing.* "*How could you?*"

Ida sobbed. "*You're punishing me. You're using her to punish me.*"

Olivia managed to compose herself. Desi's innocent face stuck in Olivia's head. Every time she closed her eyes she saw that young girl, standing there, wide-eyed and shocked. It was never her intention to put the blame for what happened on Desi. Ida had run out of the house right after it happened. She'd left them both standing there, Desi and Olivia, and Julian lying bleeding on the floor.

"They'll kill her," Olivia said, softly. "She'll get the death penalty. You know she will."

Ida broke down crying even harder. "Lord! No! No!"

"Or she could serve time," Olivia continued. I don't know how long, but, at least if she serves time, she can come out someday."

Ida shook her head. "She can't go to prison! Desi can't—"

"Neither can I! I'd die in a place like that!"

"And she won't?"

"She's young, Ida," Olivia argued. "Trust me when I tell you that the only two options for Desi are the death penalty, or to serve time. It's already been decided. It's done. But I can make sure she doesn't get the death penalty. And I can promise you that she can have the money."

Everyone had a price. Ida Green was no different. Julian had thought he'd hidden it well enough that Olivia would never find out about it. When a rich man dies, the question of his money comes into play even before they put him in the ground. The attorneys found every last cent, even what he'd hidden in his mother's name and flowed down to the bogus entity that led straight to Ida.

"Think about what I'm saying," Olivia begged. "Think about it. Your daughter could die, and you'll lose absolutely everything."

Ida fell to the floor on her knees.

"Or, she can serve a prison sentence. She loses some years, but she still has a chance at her life. She can get out and rebuild with the money that Julian left you. She can start over. But you have to promise not to tell anyone about me. You have to promise to keep this secret, Ida, and to see to it that Desi keeps it,

or I swear, she won't ever get out of prison alive. It's done. The trial hasn't started, and I know how this will end. I already know, Ida."

That was the day that Ida sold her daughter to her fate, or she bought her from it. It was hard to say.

Trouble in Mind

"A football." Lonnie held the pigskin in front of her with the tips of her fingers as if it was covered in slime. She looked at Jordan who'd told her he had a surprise for her. He'd brought her out to the park, pulled a football out of his trunk, and handed it to her.

"That looks good on you," he grinned.

"What am I supposed to do with it?"

He took it from her hands. "Go long?"

Lonnie looked like he'd spoken to her in German. "What?"

"Run!"

Lonnie took off like he'd fired a gun into the air, and moments later the ball goes whizzing by her head. She ducked and screamed. He chased her down, scooped her up, and spun her around.

"Are you trying to kill me?" Lonnie yelled. "Do I look like Tim Tebow to you?"

"No, thank God!"

It was the first time she'd ever seen him like this. Relaxed, playful, running around her like a little kid. Even naked, Jordan was an imposing and sophisticated figure. That afternoon, he'd been transported back to a time in his life when he wasn't in charge of an empire. He was just some guy.

Jordan and Lonnie lay spread out on a blanket, drinking wine, and feeding each other fruit and cheese. "So, you falling for me yet?"

Lonnie laughed. "I fell for you a long time ago."

"I'm serious."

"I thought you said I didn't have to."

"When did I say that?"

"You said I didn't have to love you back."

"So, that means you don't plan on it?"

"You lied to me."

"I did. I admit it. I figured I'd give you a few days, and you'd come around."

Lonnie laughed. "Then you don't know me at all."

"Oh, I know you better than you give me credit for, Yolanda."

"I certainly hope not."

It was such a beautiful day. Claire raised her face to the sun and let the warmth wash over her. Of course he was here. Claire could smell him in the air, she could feel him in the sun. Jordan was the whole world to her.

"Hey! Are you alright? Lady?"

"What was tha—Jordan?" She heard him. "Jord . . ."

"What the hell is wrong . . ."

He didn't know. He didn't know how much he meant to her. He

didn't know how deeply she loved him. Jordan didn't listen. He was too busy. Always too busy.

"Meghan! Come here! Come to Mommy!"

"What's wrong with that lady?"

"Come on!"

There . . . Of course it was him. The image of him blurred behind her tears, but she'd come out here to show him how much she loved him, and how hurt she felt when he broke her heart. All she wanted was to make him happy, to have his children. All she wanted was to be the wife he told her he'd wanted back when they were dating. He'd wanted her so much back then. He would call her at all hours, take her on exotic trips, bought her nice things.

"Claire?"

He was with some slut. He was with . . . with . . .

"Claire? What the hell did you do?"

"Oh my God!"

"Shut up!" Claire screamed at her. "Shut up! That's my husssban! My . . . husssban . . . Jordan!"

Could he see? Could he see now?

"Call 9-1-1!" Jordan called out.

The sun must've started to go down. It was getting so dark . . . so fast.

Jordan came to her. Claire held out her arms to embrace him. "Baby," she sobbed. He could see, finally. He could finally see her love.

Claire had slit her wrists. Jordan and Lonnie watched shocked as the paramedics loaded her into the back of the ambulance. He could smell the alcohol on her breath.

"I've gotta go," he said to Lonnie.

"Go," she insisted.

"Can you get home alright?" he asked climbing into the back of the ambulance.

"I'll be fine. Just go."

It was late. Jordan was exhausted. Claire was stable and when he left, she was sleeping. He should've gone home, but home was the last place he wanted to be. Without even thinking about it, he ended up parked outside the building Lonnie lived in. He needed to talk. That's all. Just to . . .

A ghost-gray Aston Martin pulled up to the front door. The windows were rolled down and he watched Lonnie and Desi talking in the car for several minutes before Lonnie finally got out and went inside.

"I'll be damned," he muttered, dismally.

A Beautiful Tale A Beautiful Tale

Nobody

"*Shocking footage* surfaced on YouTube today of a brutal beating of a young man at the hands of a man who appears to be a federally appointed judge from the small, northeast Texas community of Blink. Authorities immediately removed the video from the Internet site, and have taken it into evidence. We have a clip of the incident, but must warn you that the scene is very graphic, and some viewers may find it offensive. The young man in the video is believed to be fifteen-year-old Aaron Baker, reported missing several months ago by his grandmother in Louisiana. There is also speculation that the body found two weeks ago in Pearsall, Texas could be that of Aaron Baker."

Delilah sat across from him in the interrogation room, looking as white as a ghost. Her eyes were bloodshot and swollen, and she stared at Russ like she didn't even know him. There was no fight left in him.

Russ felt every bit his age and then some. He was numb inside and out. The evidence against him was insurmountable, and he knew that it was only a matter of hours before they confirmed that the body they'd found belonged to Aaron.

"H-how long have you been . . ." Delilah couldn't bring herself to say something she didn't understand.

"It's not what you think," Russ said despondently. It was what he was supposed to say, rehearsed and scripted. But he didn't mean a word of it. So, how could he possibly think he could convince her?

"He was just a boy, Russ." Her voice quivered. "Our boys . . ."

Her implication shot a bolt of lightning straight through him. "I never laid a finger on our boys!" he shouted angrily. "Never! And don't you dare sit there and accuse me either!" Russ composed himself then deflated again in his chair. "I thought he was nineteen," he lied.

He told himself that's what that boy was, that that's what they all were, but Russ was forced to come to terms with the truth now. They were young. All of them were too young.

"Wasn't I enough, Russ?" Delilah sobbed. "I thought I was enough."

His heart went out to her, and broke in two. How could he ever make her understand that this had nothing to do with her? How could he convince her that he loved her now as much as the day they were married, and that he always would?

"It wasn't you, honey," he said, hoping she would believe him. "It was me. It was always me, Delilah."

"And Tom?" She choked back tears. "Was what they said about him true too?"

Russ let his eyes close, and nodded.

"Then shame on both of you." Delilah shook her head. "Shame on you. Weren't you the one who said people who break the law just get what they deserve?"

"She saw to it that we did," he admitted solemnly.

"W-who?"

He sighed. "Desi Green. She did this to me—to Tom."

Delilah frowned. "No, Russ. No! You did this to yourself! You went to that place and molested young boys!" Delilah stood up and pointed her finger in his face. "You beat that boy until he was dead! And then you hid him out there in the middle of nowhere! You used him and you threw him away! You can't blame anybody else for this!" An officer came into the room and pulled her out. "You can't blame anybody for this but your damn self!"

Desi watched that video, horrified. He was so young. He was a child.

"The boy didn't put the camera in the room," Lonnie had told her. "Management did. They filmed all the clients in all the rooms. And they had more than one camera."

"Why?" she asked.

"Leverage." She shrugged. "Money."

"How'd you get this tape, Lonnie?"

She looked at her. "I've got my sources."

Desi picked up the phone and called Lonnie. "You see the news?"

Lonnie sighed. "I saw it. You still think we should've waited and let that bastard walk around free to do that to another kid?"

"He deserves to be buried under the fuckin' jail," Desi muttered. "Even that's too good for him."

"He's going to finally get what's coming to him, Des. Shit, he was worse than the criminals he convicted."

Lonnie was right.

"His self-righteous ass had no business being a judge."

"He's sitting on the other side of the fence now. But I've got to give it to him. At least he didn't go out like Billings."

I Seen Rain

"*I need to see you!*" Never in a million years would Fleming think he'd be making demands on Gatewood, but he had no choice. Neither one of them had a choice. Fleming was desperate. They'd kill him in prison, but only if he went to prison. Russ needed to somehow beat this, and the only option he had left was with Gatewood money.

"You need to lose this number," Jordan retorted.

Russ spoke quickly, before Gatewood hung up on him. "And you need to get down here before I start spilling my guts, telling the truth about your father's murder."

The line didn't go dead. Obviously, Russ had his attention.

"There are some things you don't know," Russ continued, struggling to get his composure in line. "Things we kept from you back then. Important details about the night he was shot."

"There's nothing more I fuckin' need to know, Fleming."

"There's plenty you need to know, Jordan." Russ's heart raced, and sweat beaded across his forehead. "Things we kept hidden, that could destroy what's left of the Gatewood foundation if it gets out. So, if I were you, I'd bust my ass to get down here as soon as possible, or I'll tell everybody within earshot what I know, including the authorities and the media."

"Tell me now!" Jordan demanded.

"I tell you face-to-face, or you find out about it the same way everybody else does, in Desi Green's book."

"What the hell do you know?"

"Like I said, I'll tell you when you get here. And bring the name and number of a good lawyer, the best your money can buy."

Russ slammed the receiver down on the hook and then he crossed his fingers, said a silent prayer, and hoped to God that he'd planted that seed of urgency deep in the man's head.

Russ had held up his end of that twenty-six-year-old bargain. He'd kept his mouth shut, saw to it that Desi Green was convicted, and still managed to keep the death penalty out of the mix.

"Of course I have to sentence her to death," Russ argued. *"We're talking murder one for crying out loud. How the hell do you expect me to sell a sentence without the words 'lethal injection' attached?"*

"I don't want her to die! And that's all I'm going to say about it!"

"I don't know how to swing it! People are going to be calling for her head on a platter!"

"Give him more money."

Lawyers looked at each other, then they both stared at her, Olivia Gatewood, who hadn't taken her eyes off Russ since she'd walked into the room.

"Mrs. Gatewood—"

"Promise me you'll let her live," she barked. *"Promise me, Fleming!"*

He made that promise, and she made sure those high-powered attorneys of hers filled up her bank account.

He'd kept her secret, and he'd kept Desi Green alive, a decision every last one of them were probably regretting right about now. The rest of them had given up, or given in to guilt. Mary Travis rotted away in guilt, Billings killed himself out of fear, but Russ wasn't going to curl up and die. He'd bent over backward and sideways for the Gatewoods, compromising his bench, his integrity. The money they paid him was nothing to those people, but it had been a fortune to him. Junior was worth twice as much as his father had been. He could afford the best attorney money could buy, and Russ needed the best. Gatewood would help him get it.

That bastard Fleming looked like he'd shit his pants if you sneezed. Jail wasn't a good fit on him, and life in a federal penitentiary would be even worse. Jordan doubted the man would be able to survive a single night in the pen.

Jordan had driven an hour and a half to Larimer County to sit across a table from Fleming. "I'm waiting," he said, coolly.

"Before I start," the judge said, nervously, "I need your word that you'll get me a lawyer, and a damn good one, Jordan. My life is on the line here, and I can't have anything less than the best."

Jordan sat as still as a statue.

"Please," Russ said, nervously. "You get me a lawyer, a team of lawyers to help me beat this, and I'll drop a bomb on you that'll blow your mind."

"Like I said, I'm listening."

Confusion and desperation flashed on Fleming's face.

"The night your father was killed, there were three women in that room."

Three? Jordan had never heard about a third woman.

"Desi, her mother Ida." The judge's hand shook as he raked it over his balding head. "Desi, her mother, Ida, and Mrs. Gatewood, your mother." The judge's hand shook as he raked it over his balding head. "Desi didn't shoot Gatewood," he reluctantly admitted.

"Desi shot him. The first officer on the scene testified that he saw her holding the gun in her hand."

"Because one of the other women put it there. This woman shot him, and panicked, and then shoved the weapon in Desi's hands, moments before the police busted into the place."

Jordan started to process what Russ was telling him, but it didn't make sense. Desi shot Julian. Either Russ was lying, or—

"Which was the woman?"

Russ paused, swallowed. "Olivia Gatewood," he finally said.

Jordan sat there watching the man's lips move, but the name didn't register.

"Your mother shot and killed your father, Jordan."

"You can't prove that," Jordan argued defiantly.

"Ida and Desi were both witnesses. Olivia's prints were on that gun along with Desi's."

Jordan clenched his jaws, and was about to get up and leave.

"She was at that house, Jordan! She found out about your father's affair, found out where his girlfriend lived, and she went there to confront him, both of them."

"The gun belonged to Ida Green!" Jordan argued.

"Ida Green didn't own a gun! It was your father's gun, registered in his name. Olivia brought it with her, probably to shoot Ida, but she shot her husband instead."

No. No, that couldn't be true. This asshole had to have been lying. Olivia wouldn't hurt a fly. She was the victim in all this. She loved Julian, and there's no way in hell she'd have shot him.

"She's the reason Desi didn't get the death penalty," Russ continued, pleading with his eyes for Jordan to believe him. "She begged me not to sentence her to death, even paid me another fifty thousand so that I would promise not to do it. You know me, son. I'll give a man the death penalty for jaywalking and not give it a second thought."

Desi spent twenty-five years in prison for nothing? For Olivia? All sorts of questions began tumbling over each other in his mind. He'd never understood why the judge hadn't sentenced a convicted killer to death. During the trial, he couldn't understand Ida Green's vague recollection of what had happened that night, unless—

"The money," Jordan suddenly said. "Ida Green's money. My mother claimed that the accountants didn't know that millions of dollars were missing."

"They knew, Jordan. Olivia knew, and she let Ida keep it, in exchange for her and Desi's silence. I don't know the details of the conversation the two of them had, but your mother knew about that money."

Jordan felt as if the floor had dropped out from underneath him.

"You were so young back then," Russ explained. "Too young to understand."

He'd understood some things, like paying off jurors to make sure Desi's verdict came back guilty. They'd explained that to him, and Jordan had agreed to it, but that's because he believed that she was guilty. But, even if he hadn't believed it, even if he'd known the truth, would he have done anything any differently?

Fleming nervously wrung his hands together. "So you see, son . . ." He swallowed and cleared his throat. "You can't leave me in here with what I know. Bail's set at two million," he continued, apprehensively. "I have been loyal to your family."

Jordan showed no emotion. "For a price, Russ."

Fleming shrugged. "If I weren't afraid for my life, I wouldn't have asked you to come. I need. . . . You have to get me out, Jordan." Russ had said all he needed to say.

Jordan stood up to leave. "I'll make arrangements."

Russ took a much-needed deep breath as he watched Gatewood leave, relieved and certain that he'd be out by morning.

Blues for Mama

Solomon had decided to take a chance and stop by without calling first. Lately, every time he had called, he spent more time having a conversation with Desi's voice mail than with her.

When she answered the door, he'd forgotten all about feeling slighted and being angry that she'd been ignoring him for the last week. Desi smiled, stepped aside, and ushered him in. On the way, he stole a kiss.

"I'm surprised you're still up," he said, stepping into the main living room and making himself comfortable on the sofa. Desi sat on his lap.

"Me, too. It's way past my bedtime."

He'd have loved to just go upstairs and crawl into bed with her, but Solomon had to get his head out of the clouds and follow through with the reason he'd come here in the first place.

"Where've you been?"

"Rodanthe, North Carolina," Desi said, proudly. "Sue Parker, the writer, has a beach house out there and we thought it would be a nice, quiet spot to work on the book."

"Was it?"

"It was amazing, Solomon. You ever been to the Outer Banks?"

"Can't say that I have."

"I'm thinking of buying a place out there. The sunrises were beautiful." Desi's eyes lit up as she talked about the place.

"I'll definitely have to check it out."

"You should. I think you'd love it."

"You couldn't have told me that you were leaving?"

Desi looked uncomfortable. "I didn't know that I needed to."

"It would've been the considerate thing to do, Desi."

He could tell he'd struck a nerve, a defensive one.

"So, did you come out here to cuss me out or something?"

"I've called quite a few times."

"I know."

"I was hoping we could talk."

She smiled. "We're talking now."

"I want to understand what you're doing." He asked, seriously.

"Right now? I'm sitting on your lap in my living room."

"You getting back at them?" He continued. "Is that what this is about?"

"Back at who, Solomon?" she asked, irritated.

"I'm not blind, Desi, and I'm not stupid. First Billings, and now Fleming? And Mary."

"What about them?"

"All these people, dropping like flies. All of them in one way or another connected to you and that trial. If I can see it, so can everybody else."

"What do you expect me to say?"

"Did you kill Julian?"

He could tell from the look on her face that she hadn't expected him to ask the question. Desi pursed her lips together and then finally made her confession. "No."

He had to process this. Of course when he'd asked that question, the answer could've gone either way. Logically, with everything he'd pieced together, it made more sense she had been innocent. But it was still a huge pill to swallow, because it meant that an entire system had caved in on her and failed miserably. Leaving in its place a woman whose only idea of justice meant lowering herself to their level and allowing herself to act as despicably as they had.

"What you're doing isn't right, Desi. I know it may feel right, but it's not, baby. You don't go around digging up shit on people to use it against them and get revenge on them."

She stared unemotionally at him. "If I don't do it, who will?"

"The law," he said, without hesitating.

Desi laughed.

Cup of Sorrow

Jordan stood on the top level of the deck watching his mother humming to herself and swirling around in her garden as if she was dancing in a ballroom. Whatever was going on in her head, she believed it was real. Jordan watched in awe as she laughed, stopped from time to time, and appeared to chat with someone who was nothing more than a memory.

The walls of that small jail cell were really starting to close in on Russ Fleming. He missed Delilah, but she hadn't come by to see him since right after he'd been arrested. He'd tried calling, but she hadn't accepted his calls. He was counting on Gatewood to get him what he needed, bail and one hell of a law team, who could pull rabbits out of hats, and make that tape inadmissible at trial.

Too much was happening too fast and all at once. When had he stopped paying attention? Claire was out of the hospital and had moved back home with her parents. The divorce papers were in the process of being prepared. *Irreconcilable differences.* He'd taken the liberty of saving her the trouble of filing them and had made arrangements to give her 10 percent more than what the prenup called for and the house if she wanted it, for her troubles. It was the least he could do.

Russ had lost control. That boy didn't have to die, and he knew that. He'd punished himself for it time and time again, since it had happened. He'd made a mistake, panicking when he found out that he had been filmed, and he took it out on the boy. He was scared that his secret would get back to Delilah, to hell with everybody else. But the last person he wanted to know about the things he did, was her. Delilah was his world. He'd loved her since they were freshmen in high school, and if it ever got back to her, what he was doing, it would've killed her, and that had just about killed him.

Two plus two equaled Lonnie and Desi. He still didn't know how that union had come about, but the fact remained that they knew each other and probably had since before he'd met Lonnie. It was impossible for him not to feel set up. Seeing the two of them together completed the puzzle. Lonnie had had his cell number and e-mail address. And somehow, she'd discovered something that she and Desi were holding over his head, or so they thought. Any other man might have felt heartache. Jordan wasn't any other man.

"Fleming." The officer came over to his cell and unlocked the door. "You've got a phone call."

Russ's eyes lit up. "My wife?"

"Don't know," he said unemotionally.

It had to be her. And if it wasn't, he didn't care to talk to anyone else, except Gatewood, or lawyers he'd found for him. Maybe that's who it was. Russ had a lawyer of his own, but the man wasn't savvy enough to handle this type of case. He hurried out of the cell, and followed the officer down the hall.

Russ Fleming was a drowning man, a desperate one who was willing to take down the whole ship to save himself. He could've told Jordan that the sky was falling and Jordan would have believed that, but to tell him that Olivia had been the one to murder Julian . . .

Olivia danced barefoot in the grass, laughing, with her face turned up to the sun. She looked happy, and whole. She looked radiant. Jordan couldn't help but smile. Maybe she was better off, he thought sadly. She could remember Julian in a better light, and she could remember how he had loved her, and what the future held for both of them. She could grow old with her husband.

"I don't understand," Russ said, nervously looking at the officers filling the room. "I was told I had a phone call."

They never said a word to him. He watched in amazement, speechless as they began pulling their batons from their holsters.

"I-I was told I had a phone—"

The first blow whipped across his shoulders on his back. The next one landed hard on the back of his knee, forcing him to crumple to the floor.

He thought Delilah had called. He thought maybe his lawyers would call.

The pain was excruciating, blinding, his own screams echoed in his head, as he melted into the floor.

Olivia finally stopped dancing, gazed up at Jordan standing on the deck, and put her hand above her eyes to shield them from the sun.

"Julian!" She smiled. "Is that you? Hey there, honey!"

Jordan smiled. "It's me, sugah," he said. "It's the man of your dreams."

She laughed. "You're so silly!" She laughed. "Silly man!"

Russ couldn't walk. They dragged him to the infirmary, and told the nurses something to the effect that he got into a fight with another inmate—and lost. They all laughed. Russ couldn't open his eyes. The scent of blood filled his nostrils. There wasn't a muscle on his body that didn't hurt, and it hurt to take a deep breath. Delilah wasn't going to call him ever again. And Gatewood wasn't sending any lawyers. But he had sent a message, and Russ got it, loud and clear.

Jordan looked at his watch. One down. Two to go.

This Dance Will Be Ending

"*What the hell* is this, Lonnie?"

Lonnie had been wanting to tell Desi this part. This was the hard part.

"What's it look like?"

Desi studied the documents lying on the table in front of her. "How'd you get Jordan Gatewood's birth certificate?"

"Certificates." Lonnie corrected her. "Look again."

Desi looked at both of them again, more carefully. "Who's Joel Tunsen?" she asked, looking at Lonnie. "Julian's name is on this one? Lonnie?"

"Look at the dates. One is dated three months earlier. Olivia and Julian had the birth certificate changed, Desi. He wasn't Julian's biological son. A man named Joel Tunsen is his father. And please don't ask me if I'm sure. Just, trust me. Julian may have been your father, but not his."

Desi looked at the photocopy of the photograph. "Is this Olivia Gate-wood?" she asked, referring to the woman.

"And the man next to her is Joel Tunsen. Can you see the resemblance?"

The pain in Desi's eyes was undeniable. Lonnie had expected to be able to gloat over this revelation. She'd expected to feel like she'd won the lottery when she gave Desi this news. But no matter how hard she looked, Lonnie could find no victory in this.

"Does he know?"

Lonnie shook her head. "I don't think so."

Desi had to sit back and let it all sink in. "My God, Lonnie," her voice cracked. "Just when I think there can't be anything else . . ."

"I know, Des," Lonnie said, sadly. "I know."

"This whole time—this whole goddamned. How did you get these? And don't tell me you got them from a source."

"That's exactly where I got them, Desi, and the source is Olivia Gate-wood's private nurse."

Tears started to flow fast and furious down Desi's cheeks. "Shit. Shit. Shit. Damn, Lonnie!"

Lonnie came over to Desi and hugged her. Instead of this being the big finale she'd hoped for, all it had really done was break Desi's heart. And it had broken Lonnie's in a way she hadn't expected. It was one thing to catch the bad guys, like Billings and Fleming. But this was different.

Contrary to what she had been trying to tell herself, Lonnie did care about Jordan, and she doubted seriously that Jordan knew that Julian wasn't his father. But when he found out the truth, and he would, she knew that he'd be no better off than Desi was now. Every now and then, Lonnie came across a secret that should stay hidden where it is.

This was one of those times, because despite what she thought would happen, nobody won here.

"I'm sorry, Des."

The kid was young enough to be Jordan's son. Tall, gangly, with an Adam's apple the size of a fist and a full-blown Afro, he wasn't what Jordan had expected to find on the other end of his search. He was good. Jordan had to give him that. But he wasn't the best. Jordan had the best working for him, and he traced those e-mails Jordan had been receiving back to this guy.

He wore cool like most young men do at that age. He couldn't have been more than twenty-four, twenty-five, but he'd impressed Jordan's IT guru, Frank.

That apartment of his, if you could call it that, was no wider than Jordan's arm span. The place was little more than a closet with a bathroom. A bookcase, filled with text books, magazines, DVDs lined one wall. The other wall was filled with computer laptops, monitors, and game consoles. The place was a dump.

"Cole Masters," Jordan said as he stood over the young man sitting slumped on that dirty couch. "Is that your real name?"

Cole shrugged. "For now."

Jordan nearly smiled. The kid had swagger. It was hard not to admire swagger, even if it was young, dumb, and misplaced.

"Do you know who I am, Cole?"

The young man shrugged again, and looked bored by the question.

"You've been sending me e-mails, texts messages, and music files. Real cryptic shit. My guy had a hard time tracking it back to you. He was impressed by your skills. Since I'm not an IT guy I'm not sure what he found so impressive, but if he says you're good, that counts for something."

"So, whassup?" the kid asked, nonchalantly.

"Who put you up to sending me that shit?" Jordan asked, point-blank.

"I don't know whatcha talkin' 'bout, man."

Swagger was good in small doses, but this kid was starting to wear on his nerves.

"Think about it. Think hard."

"Man." He rolled his eyes in frustration. "I don't know, man."

Jordan circled around behind and grabbed a handful of that 'fro of his. "Motha fucka, I am not in the mood to be pissing around your sorry ass," he said menacingly. "You tell me who put your narrow ass up to sending me that shit, or I'll have that driver take your ass somewhere and lose you."

The kid looked like he didn't believe Jordan at first, so he made good on his threat, and in a motion too quick for that kid to prepare for, raised a fist over his head and brought it down hard on his bony chest.

"Man! Fuck!" The kid coughed and gasped for air. Jordan caught him by the shoulder, and forced him back down in his seat.

Jordan dug his fingers into that kid's shoulder.

"I'm going to ask one more time," he threatened. "Who put you up to this shit?"

The kid grimaced at the pain shooting down his arm and up his neck. "Let me go, dammit!"

"You answer my question, or I'll pull meat right out of this shoulder."

"Lonnie! Her name is Lonnie! That's all I know!"

Lonnie. Not Desi.

He's No Saint

She hadn't seen him since the day Claire showed up at the park, but they'd spoken on the phone and he'd told her that Claire had left him. Lonnie wasn't the kind of woman to jump to conclusions. Claire's leaving was exactly what it was and nothing more. It didn't make room for Lonnie and Jordan to be together. If he thought that, then he was wrong.

She'd reluctantly agreed to let him pick her up. Dinner he said. When she got into the car, they didn't even kiss.

"It's good to see you," he said, forcing a smile.

"You too," she nodded.

"I hope you're hungry."

"Famished."

"Not cool, Jordan," Lonnie said, shakily. "Not cool!"

He'd brought her to a small bungalow he owned in the middle of nowhere. "What's not cool is you setting me up, Lonnie."

She was afraid of him. Jordan stalked her through each room, tossing furniture aside like the Hulk, trying to back her into a corner.

"I didn't set you up!"

Jordan's eyes bore holes into her. "You tried to make a fool out of me."

"What? You're crazy!"

"I am now, yeah. Why don't you tell me the truth, for once?"

"About what?" She made the mistake of not paying attention and backing up into a corner.

He pushed against her. "About Desi Green?" He blocked her in, bracing both arms around her.

Lonnie was speechless.

"What? The two of you met in prison?"

"No," she whispered, caught off guard that he'd figured out that the two of them knew each other.

"You set me up, Lonnie."

Lonnie felt herself tremble. "That's not how it was, Jordan," she said, trying not to sound as afraid as she was. Big, bad Lonnie wasn't feeling so big and bad now. Jordan was a bull and he was pissed.

"How was it, Lonnie?" He tapped her in the face with the flat of his hand.

"Don't you dare hit me!" she said, pointing her finger in his face.

He slapped it away. "You set me up? You got something on me?"

The wild look in his eyes was frightening.

"No!"

"You sending me texts and e-mails, Lonnie. Got your little friend, what's his name, Cole something-or-other, sending shit to my personal number."

How did he find out about . . .

"I am not the idiot you thought I was, bitch."

Lonnie tried to get away from him. Jordan grabbed her, and shoved her back against the wall.

"You like it rough, don't you, baby?" He grabbed her by the back of the neck, forced her across the room and over to the dining table.

"Stop it!"

Jordan forced her facedown onto the table, bending her over it. "Let's play, Lonnie. We got the place all to our self, and we got all night, baby girl!"

Lonnie fought him. She screamed and cried out for help until the truth finally hit her that nobody could hear her.

The sun was starting to come up. Jordan stepped outside, took a deep breath, and made a phone call. "I need you to come out to the Bankfield house and clean up something for me." He hung up.

He noticed blood on the hem of his shirt. Jordan peeled out of it, opened the door, and tossed it inside. Men like him didn't get their hands dirty on shit like this, but it was personal this time. Even more personal than Desi Green. He'd never said anything he didn't mean. He'd told the woman he'd loved her and he had loved her. Lonnie was one of a kind. She was the yin to his yang.

"Too bad," he said, clearing his throat. Too bad things between them didn't turn out the way he'd hoped it would.

Blue Prelude

Not many pretty young girls walked up to him purposefully anymore. This one was fine, could've been thicker, but nice. She walked over to him, watching him watering his garden. He figured that maybe she was lost, and needed directions. He knew Texas like the back of his hand, so he'd help her if he could.

"Mr. Tunson?" the young woman asked, wearily.

He stared at her and nodded. "That's me," he said, suspiciously. "Who you?"

"My name's Desi Green."

Nice enough name. It suited her. "You here to see that boy of mine?"

Now, he knew what the boy's problem was. And why he slept all the damn time, and stayed out all night. This pretty thing right here, was taking his mind off the things it should've been on, like getting to work on time, saving his money, and settling down.

"No, sir," she said, softly. "I came to see you."

Joel nearly shit his pants when she said that. She looked like she wore most of her money on her back. Joel quickly sized her up and determined that she was a bill collector of some sort, or maybe she was selling insurance.

"Whatever you selling, I ain't interested," he said, gruffly.

"I'm not selling anything," she assured him. "But I would like to ask you a few questions, if you have time."

Her voice sounded as sweet as bells. He looked into those pretty brown eyes, and fell in love just that quick. If he were a younger man, this one here would be in trouble. But since he was old now, she had nothing to worry about. He turned off his hose, and led her over to the front porch of his house.

"You from around here?" he asked, as they were sitting down.

"No, sir, well—I'm from Blink, which is close enough, I guess."

"I know Blink," he said, unemotionally. "Got a few cousins up that way. What's your last name again?" he asked, eyeing her. Maybe she was related.

"Green," she said.

Joel thought long and hard. "Naw. Don't know no Greens. So, what is it you wanna ask me?"

Desi reached into her purse and pulled out the photograph Lonnie had given her. "Is that you in this picture?"

He adjusted his glasses on his nose, and then pulled them off altogether, stretched out his arm, stared at it, and started to grin. "That sho' is me." He laughed. "Me and Olivia Franklin," he boasted. "And my old Buick. Damn! I loved that car." He looked at Desi. "Where'd you get this?"

"A friend of mine gave it to me."

He studied Desi. "Where'd they get it?"

"I honestly don't know."

"So, why you showing it to me?"

She didn't look like Joel but that didn't mean she wasn't one of his. Back when he was young, he was wild, sticking his thing in places it didn't belong, so there was no doubt in his mind that he could've had kids coming out of the corners like roaches.

"You remember Olivia Franklin?" she probed carefully.

He looked at Desi like she was crazy. "What man in his right mind would ever forget Olivia Franklin? She was the finest thing on two legs for damn near five counties. So, yes. I remember Olivia Franklin."

"How well did you know her?"

He frowned. "Whatchu mean how well? I knew her well enough."

"Well enough to have a baby by her?"

All that spit and fire disappeared from him, and Joel Tunson felt like he was about to be sick.

"Who are you and why you asking me all these questions?"

"I think I know your son," she said cautiously.

He turned his head and stared out into the yard. Joel had sons. He had four of them, one living up the road, the other one married and living in Jacksonville, Florida. One asleep in the back room and one, well, he wasn't sure where that last one was.

"Jordan Gatewood?" she continued, cautiously. "Does that name ring a bell?"

Of course it did. That name made him want to spit, and cuss, and throw his fist into something hard.

"Who sent you here?" he asked, defiantly.

"No one." She swallowed. "I came because I need to know if you really are Jordan's father."

"Why are you here, and not him?" He was angry. That boy should've been down here asking these questions. Not her. Not anybody else. Just him.

"Because I don't think he wants to know," she admitted.

Joel's feelings were hurt. But if it was the truth, he appreciated it being the truth.

"Olivia was too pretty for any man, except a rich one," he began to explain. "Her daddy never did think much of me, 'cause I work with my hands and my back. I couldn't even pick her up at her house. She'd meet me at the five-and-dime, I'd pick her up in my car, even taught her how to drive, and we'd roll off someplace and just have a good time."

"How old was she?"

"Twenty, twenty-one. Somewhere in there."

"She had to sneak around at twenty-one?"

"That's how it was, girl. I didn't mind so much until she told me about the baby." He looked briefly at Desi. "I wanted to be a father, and since she was carrying my child, I knew I needed to marry her. So, I went to her door, knocked on it, and asked to speak to her father."

"Was she there?"

"Yeah," he said, dismally. "She was there."

"Told him I wanted to ask for his permission to marry her. He was disgusted with her for being pregnant in the first place, said that he would've handed her over to the circus if they'd have asked for her."

"Did the two of you get married?"

He nodded. "I married her. Stayed married to her until after the baby came."

"Jordan?"

He shot an angry look at her. "Theodore," he corrected her.

Theodore?

"Named after my daddy, Theodore Jordan Tunson," he said proudly. "Olivia never liked Theodore. Changed it soon as she could."

"So, you were divorced shortly after he was born?"

"She went back home to her momma and daddy. By then, they'd forgiven her, and welcomed her home like a wayward son. Wouldn't even let me come by to see my baby. My own flesh and blood," he said, angrily. "Next thing I know, her daddy got the marriage annulled, and I got papers in the mail telling me that she was no longer my wife. I didn't have a problem with that because Olivia was one sorry-ass excuse for a wife," he fussed. "But to me, that didn't mean that my boy was no longer my boy."

"Did you ever see him again?"

He huffed. "Hell naw! Three months after she left me, she turned around and married that rich bastard, Gatewood. And they tried to act like my boy was his. Don't know what kind of trickery they used to pull that one over folks's eyes, but whatever they did it worked. He packed them both up, and took them on outta here, and I never saw either one of them again." His voice trailed off.

"Other than your word, Mr. Tunson," Desi chose her words carefully, "do you have any way of proving that Jordan—Theodore is your son?"

He looked at her, then got up and went inside the house without saying a word. A few minutes later, he came out of the house and handed her a folded-up piece of paper.

"I figure if she could take off with my son like that, then I had every right to this birth certificate. I asked the hospital for a copy right after she left me, so that I could have proof to myself that he was mine, and that I didn't make this up. I can never have him, but at least I got something."

Desi's smile lit up like it was Christmas. "Mr. Tunson, would you mind if I got a copy of this?"

"Can't nobody take that from me," he snapped.

"I don't want to take it. I just want to make a copy. You can ride with me to the library and watch me, and I'll hand it back to you as soon as I'm done."

"Whatchu need a copy for?"

"For Theodore."

Shout, Sistah! Shout!

Desi had called and left several messages for Lonnie. She'd even stopped by her place, but she didn't answer. She wanted to tell her about Tunsen, and show her the copy of the original birth certificate she'd gotten from him. Lonnie had kept both of her copies and filed them away for "safekeeping" she'd told Desi. Desi just figured that Lonnie had been called away on an assignment or something but found it strange that she hasn't even responded to email. Lonnie always answered emails.

"Where are you?" she asked Solomon over the phone.

"The office."

"Can I come by?"

"Of course you can."

"I'll be there in an hour."

"I'll be waiting."

Standing in his office, Desi was absolutely giddy.

Solomon was floored by the document he held in his hand. "Is this real?" he asked Desi, sitting on the other side of his desk in his office.

She nodded and grinned. "Got the certified seal and everything. I saw it with my own two eyes. He wouldn't part with the original, though, and damn near held me at gunpoint while I copied it, but I think it was worth it. Don't you?"

Solomon looked up at her. "What do you plan on doing with it, Desi?"

She smiled. "I plan on getting Theodore off my back."

He looked skeptical.

"You know he's not going to stop, Solomon. And when this book comes out, it's only going to get worse, unless I do something now."

He thought for a few moments before responding. "Did you put this in the book? This part about Jordan's real father?"

She shook her head. "I didn't know about it at the time. It's not in there."

He sighed. "Then I guess that's your leverage," he said, reluctantly.

She was relieved that he wasn't going to try and talk her out of it. Desi didn't need logic or reason from Solomon. She needed him to be on her side, and to understand what she understood. That Jordan Gatewood was a dirty player, who made up the rules as he went along. And the only way to play the game with someone like him, was to play it like he played it.

But there were deeper questions piquing her curiosity now since she'd gotten her hands on a copy of that birth certificate. Solomon was a lawyer, and she figured maybe he could help shine the light on some things.

"So, by birth Jordan's not a Gatewood, really."

"Not by birth. No. But Julian could've adopted him."

He could've.

"Julian was my father, Solomon," she confessed. Of course, he wouldn't believe her. And of course, she'd have to prove it, but growing up, it wasn't a secret.

Solomon stared at her. "I can imagine that he was, Desi," he said seriously. "Can you prove it?"

She gave it some thought before answering. "If it ever comes to that, then I'll try." She thought a bit more. "And if I could prove it, and prove that Jordan's not a Gatewood . . ."

Solomon smiled. "It could make for some serious legal issues."

"Meaning?"

"Meaning, he'd have a lot of explaining to do."

Desi felt smug. "Interesting."

"How many copies did you make?"

She held up her hand. "Five."

Solomon laughed. "Why so many?"

"I'm giving one to Jordan. I'm keeping one for myself. I've giving one to you. I'm putting one in a safety deposit box, and I'm sending one to Olivia Gatewood. If anything happens to me, you know what to do."

"Nothing's going to happen to you."

"But if anything ever does . . . you know what to do?"

He noded. "I know what to do."

Two days later she walked into Gatewood Tower like she owned the place, found out where Jordan's office was, and marched up to his receptionist.

"Is Mr. Gatewood in?"

"He's in a meeting. Did you have an appointment?"

"Where's the meeting?" Desi asked, boldly.

The woman looked like she didn't want to give up the information. So, Desi took the fight to another level. "I'm his sister!"

The woman looked surprised. "Oh, I'm sorry," she said, picking up the receiver to call Jordan. Desi didn't give her time to finish the call before she stormed into his office.

"What the hell?" he yelled, bolting to his feet.

She walked over to him, and tossed a copy of his birth certificate on his desk.

"Look at it," she demanded.

"You need to get your black ass out of my office!" He pointed toward the door.

"Look at it!"

He reluctantly picked up the paper she'd dropped on his desk. Jordan tossed it back at her. "What the hell is this?"

"It's your legacy, Jordan," she said, smugly.

"Bullshit." He sat down, studying the document she'd tossed at him.

"I agree, it's bullshit that you either don't know or don't want to know."

Jordan didn't turn pale, exactly, but he did turn a peculiar shade of gray as all the color left his face.

"You got a suicide wish, Desi? Because I swear. . . ."

"I met him, Jordan. Joel Tunsen. He told me all about your mother, his former wife, and the child the two of them had. He regrets that you were taken from him, but in your memory he has your birth certificate and was kind enough to let me make copies."

If he could've picked her up and thrown her out of the window of that high-rise building, he would've.

"So, is this the little project you and your friend were working on?"

"It's real. It's been certified by the state. The one with Julian's name on it was issued three months after you were born. Check it out, if you've got the guts."

"Ask Lonnie about how gutsy I can be."

Desi was shocked at hearing him mention her name. "How do you know Lonnie?"

"Oh, I know Lonnie intimately," he said, smugly.

Lonnie had never told her that she knew Jordan. She would have told Desi something like that.

"You didn't know," he laughed. "Obviously."

"She would've told me . . ."

"Not necessarily. She didn't mention you to me, either."

"You're lying, Jordan."

"What reason would I have to lie to you? Believe me, I understand your dismay. Imagine my shock and disbelief when I found out that the woman I've been fuckin all this time had you as a BFF." He leaned back and touched the tips of his fingers together.

He knew about the two of them. He knew. Desi hadn't seen or heard from Lonnie in days. Desi swallowed. "Where is she?"

He glanced at the copy of the birth certificate still on his desk. "A copy of that going in your book?"

"When's the last time you spoke to her?" she asked, apprehensively.

Jordan's expression changed. Desi couldn't read it.

"I want this to go away."

"I want you to tell me where she is!"

"You keep my shit out of your damn book."

"It'll stay out of my book, as long as you stay the hell away from me and you tell me what you've done to Lonnie!" she said, gritting her teeth.

"I can only make you one promise, that I'll stay out of your way. Nothing more."

All the air seemed to leave the room. "Where is she, Jordan," Desi whispered helplessly.

He never answered.

She turned to leave. Desi had a sick feeling in her stomach. First chance she got she was calling Lonnie again. If she didn't answer, Desi'd stop by the house again, next time with the police.

Beautiful, Dirty, Rich

Beautiful, Dirty, Rich

Beneath, Beneath the Rising

"*I didn't think* I'd have to do all this," Desi said, agitated, sitting in the back of the limousine next to Sue. "You never said anything about a book tour."

"I didn't know you'd be sent on one."

Desi's heart raced, and she felt sick to her stomach. Traffic was horrible, but it was always horrible in New York. "We're going to be late."

"For someone so against a book signing, you seem mighty anxious."

"I just want to get this over with. Nobody's going to be there."

"You might be surprised. The book's been getting a ton of press, and the reviews were remarkable, if I do say so myself." Sue patted herself on the back. "It debuted at number three on the *New York Times Bestseller* list."

Desi rolled her eyes. "Go figure."

A year had passed since Lonnie had gone missing. Desi had gone back to her condo, and when she didn't answer, called the police. There had been no sign of a struggle. Lonnie's car was parked in its designated spot. She didn't appear to have packed up and taken off on a trip or anything, there was no record of her catching a flight, and none of her friends or family had heard from her. The only image left of Lonnie was surveillance footage in the lobby of her leaving her building at seven o'clock one evening, nearly a year ago to the day.

Desi couldn't prove it, but she knew that Jordan had had something to do with her disappearance. Since the release of the book a week ago, *Beautiful, Dirty, Rich: The Desi Green Story,* he'd been out of the country. His mother, Olivia, had been checked into a nursing home where she now lived full time. Texas authorities were slow to move in and charge her with anything, because of her age and condition, and because she was Olivia Gatewood and money still talked. But even if they didn't believe Desi's claim in her book that Olivia had been the one who pulled the trigger the night Julian died, the general public and, this time, the media were on her side. Desi still hated the press, and she still refused to talk to any of them. It didn't hurt that she had exposed Billings and Fleming in her book. Out of respect for Solomon and his mother she'd left out Mary's role in the conspiracy.

This was her first official book signing at a major bookstore in Brooklyn.

"I hope no one shows up," she muttered.

"Speak for yourself," Sue said, applying lipstick.

When the driver turned the corner, both Desi and Sue sat up and gawked at the line of people waiting outside the store. Sue's face lit up. Desi felt like she wanted to vomit. "Can't you do this without me?"

Sue patted Desi on the hand. "You're the main attraction, dear. Of course I can't."

It reminded her of what it was like to be her all those years ago, when the police dragged her into and out of that courtroom in hand-cuffs. Photographers snapped pictures of her until she could hardly see from all the flashes going off in her face, hordes of people were pressed against her and they screamed at her.

"What made you do it Desi?"

"Why'd you kill him?"

"Are you afraid you'll be sent to prison?"

It seemed like a lifetime ago when she was afraid for her life, afraid they'd take it from her, and they did.

Sue squeezed her hand as the driver pulled up to the curb and stopped. "It's alright, Desi." She looked into Desi's eyes and seemed to read her mind. "It's not like before. These people aren't here to convict you again. They're here because they admire your strength for what you've been through."

Desi took a deep breath. The driver came around to open the door for them. Sue stepped out first, but when Desi stepped out, the people on line applauded.